ETERNAL CITY

ETERNAL CITY

STORIES

MOLLY SHAPIRO

Winner of the 1996 Willa Cather Fiction Prize

HELICON NINE EDITIONS
KANSAS CITY, MISSOURI

Cover design: Andrea Flamini
Cover photographs: Molly Shapiro
Book design: Tim Barnhart

The author would like to thank her family:
Alvin, Patti, Peter, Julia, Tony, Amy, and Sophie Shapiro.

Helicon Nine Editions is funded in part by
the National Endowment for the Arts, a federal agency,
and by the Missouri Arts Council and
the Kansas Arts Commission, state agencies.

Library of Congress Cataloging-in-Publication Data

Shapiro, Molly, 1967-
    Eternal city : stories / Molly Shapiro.
        p.   cm.
    Contents: Orphans -- EuroDisney -- The cooker lady -- Myanmar --
Not by choice -- Tightrope -- A violent life -- I'll see you later -- If you
were my woman -- Results -- Up and down -- Sweet tooth -- Eternal
city.

    ISBN 1-884235-21-2 : (on acid-free paper) $12.95
    I. Title.
PS3569.H34147E87 1997
813' .54--dc21
                                                              97-25509
                                                              CIP

Printed in the United States of America

First Edition

HELICON NINE EDITIONS

For Andrea

CONTENTS

ETERNAL CITY

ORPHANS

WHEN LAURA AND HENRY FIRST MOVED TO New York City seven
years ago, they thought they'd live in an artist's loft in SoHo.
They imagined themselves floating through a space unencum-
bered by walls, every inch drenched in an even yellow light which
poured from the huge windows like freshly squeezed juice from a
Lalique crystal carafe. Soon they discovered that Manhattan's
contemporary art community was full of investment bankers, fashion models, and innovative restaurateurs, but very few artists.
What a pity that such great natural light would go to waste on
people who either slept through the morning or stayed at work
until nightfall, returning to their darkened lofts only to illuminate
them with cable broadcasts and halogen.

After only a week of apartment hunting, the couple quickly
pinpointed the Lower East Side as the neighborhood which best
fit their price range. There were no stark white galleries, cozy
wood paneled bars, or bedding shops stocked with fluffy quilts and
lacy dust ruffles in this part of town, but Laura and Henry did
have to admit that the neighborhood had character. Compared to
the mild-mannered Northern California town where they both
grew up, their new home felt positively European. Their neighbors
sat on the sidewalks throughout the day, speaking in languages

Laura and Henry had never heard before. Children played in the street until they were called home by their mothers, who would suddenly appear through kitchen windows, sweaty and sticky from hours spent separating potatoes from their skins, egg yolks from their whites, and chickens from their fat.

For some reason though, this community never really warmed up to its blond-haired, blue-eyed neighbors. Every morning before they began work, Henry would go out to the corner deli for coffee and bagels, passing the Judaica shop where Mr. Weiner sold his menorahs and mezuzahs to the faithful and the faithless alike. It didn't really matter which because to him, a Jew was a Jew. But not once did Mr. Weiner ever acknowledge Henry with a good morning or even a nod. Henry wondered if perhaps the man resented Laura and him, for they represented one less menorah, one less mezuzah he could provide to a new Jewish household. Laura once suggested putting one of the more simple wooden mezuzahs up on their doorway, but they knew they couldn't pretend. It wouldn't be right to try and adopt a community with which they shared nothing but a fondness for dry baked goods. They would simply have to accept their neighbors' indifference, and wait for the day when they could move into the world in which they knew they belonged.

Laura and Henry had come to New York because they considered themselves serious artists. Not content to support a peaceful, bucolic existence by setting up stands at craft fairs and local art shows, they decided to move to the center of contemporary art. They aspired to more than just decorating waterfront homes and mountain retreats. They wanted to be a part of history.

Laura was a painter and Henry a sculptor, and they used their relatively spacious living room as their studio, filling it with paints and canvases, clay and podiums stacked with sculptures. Laura tried to keep the kitchen free from toxic pigments and mineral spirits, but it was difficult, and she often found herself chopping carrots with knives which had once carved the delicate lines of a woman's lips. For seven years they had lived in that apartment, never able to afford a bigger, nicer place, not even when they got married during their second year in their new home.

Every day from nine to six, Laura and Henry worked in their studio. At night they worked at a Mexican restaurant in the East Village where she waitressed and he was a cook. They were just barely able to make enough money to pay the rent and bills, buy food and art supplies, so they did their best to save money any way they could. They avoided taking the subway by only going places where they could walk, and instead of buying the newspaper, they got their daily news from the public radio station.

On Fridays they took the day off and went to SoHo to see the galleries. Every week they would go into the same galleries, with the same young, well-groomed men and women sitting at the front desks. They were so good-looking, those gallery assistants, people of unique ethnicities, the offspring of unions between Eskimos, Filipinos, Italians, Native Americans, Afro-Americans and Dutch. But never did they seem to recognize Laura and Henry. Every Friday, the couple would shyly approach the desk, look casually at the price lists, then wander around the gallery staring at the works of art. Yet they were paid no more attention than the middle-aged man and wife with the matching fur coats, the gay couple from Lincoln, Nebraska, or the students from the local art school who carried boxes of pencils and big pads of newsprint. Laura and Henry were actually quite grateful for their anonymity, for they dreaded the day when someone might recognize them as the couple who had been submitting slides every March and September for the past seven years.

Ever since they first arrived in New York, Henry and Laura had alternated sending slides of their work to the various galleries around town. If Henry sent his slides in March, Laura would wait till September to send hers. While this system originated because of the high costs of slide making and postage, the couple found that it was also ideal in lessening the amount of rejection they would have to endure. This way, Laura could open Henry's packets of slides, and place the accompanying letter in the appropriate file. Six months later, Henry could do the same for her. They never even considered not sending out their work. It was something they felt they had to do, if only to remain somehow connected to the world of contemporary art.

Because gallery browsing was so exhausting and there was never anywhere to sit inside the huge, white spaces, Laura and Henry would always take a long, leisurely lunch break at one of the local cafés. They would each order English Breakfast tea and then split a sandwich. The sandwiches were made on hard French rolls and filled sparingly with things like roasted eggplant, sun-dried tomatoes, buffalo mozzarella, or arugula. Laura and Henry tried to ignore the fact that the sandwiches cost six or seven dollars, and ate them slowly, savoring the sometimes delicate, sometimes robust flavors. They knew they could have gotten a couple slices of pizza for less, but they liked this café with its white tiled floors, jet-black trim, and marble table tops. On Fridays, they couldn't resist catering to their every esthetic need.

While Henry rarely talked to his family in California, Laura spoke to her mother almost every week. Henry came from a large family of seven and it seemed to him that his parents were quite content to speak to him on his birthday, Christmas, and little else. He guessed they had enough kids to keep track of on their own coast. Laura, on the other hand, was an only child and since her mother was a widow, Laura was all she had. Her mother worked for a health care company as a receptionist, and although she barely made enough money to maintain herself, she was always asking Laura if she could send her some extra cash.

"Just a couple hundred. So you can get yourself something nice."

"No, Mom, really. I won't take your money," said Laura.

And it was true. A few times Laura's mother had sent her checks for one, two hundred dollars and they promptly came back to her with "Void" scrawled across the front. Laura was determined to make it on her own.

"Listen, Laura. I talked to that Jeannie Carroway again. You know, the one that used to work in the Marketing Department?"

"Mom, I'm really not interested."

"But she wants to see your work and who knows, maybe she'll

8

buy something. She certainly has enough money."

"You don't understand, Mom. It just doesn't work that way. Anyway, I guarantee she won't be interested in my stuff."

"Please, Laura. Give it a try."

"Whatever."

At one time, Laura and Henry had been all too willing to welcome interested strangers into their studio, but quickly they realized that contemporary art was not meant for the masses. While they had thought that masters like Pollack and Picasso, Moore and Miro had rescued all future artists from listening to painful laments like: "I don't see what's so difficult about that," they found that not since the Renaissance had the general public's relationship to art taken any further steps toward understanding.

And yet when Mrs. Jeannie Carroway called one Wednesday morning to see if she could come by the studio Saturday afternoon, Laura found herself oddly accommodating.

"Do you mind if I make myself scarce?" asked Henry when he heard the news.

"Not at all," said Laura. "Why should both of us suffer."

"I thought maybe I'd go do some shopping."

"Shopping?"

"Our fifth anniversary's coming up," said Henry.

"I know," said Laura. "But please, Henry, don't go spending money on presents."

"Don't worry. Nothing big."

Laura felt bad. She hoped she hadn't spoiled Henry's plans. She should have just trusted him. He knew what they could afford and what they couldn't.

When the doorbell rang at three o'clock, Laura went downstairs to let Mrs. Carroway in.

"Laura, it's so nice to finally meet you. You look just like your mother, that sweet woman."

The two walked slowly up the dark, damp steps, Jeannie Carroway doing her best to keep her shiny, black sable coat from touching the walls. Once they reached the open door of the apartment, Mrs. Carroway's eyes widened.

"Oh my."

"Sorry for the mess."

"Oh no, it's wonderful. Like a real artist's studio."

Laura wondered why this was "like" a real artist's studio and not actually a real one itself.

"It's simply marvelous!" Mrs. Carroway walked over to one of Henry's sculptures. "Do you sculpt as well?"

"Oh no, that's my husband's work."

"Your husband's an artist, too? Oh, how adorable!"

Laura felt her teeth clench. "Well, it would probably be even more adorable if we were both lawyers," she said.

"Oh, I know. It must be so difficult for you both." Mrs. Carroway was suddenly stricken with sympathy.

"Whatever. We survive." Laura didn't want to get too intimate with Jeannie Carroway.

Determined to get this meeting over with, Laura ushered Mrs. Carroway over to the three paintings which hung on the large wall opposite the windows. She particularly wanted to show Mrs. Carroway these paintings first, for they were her strongest, harshest, most daring works yet. Laura hoped she might be able to scare Jeannie Carroway off. Each canvas depicted a child, but not the innocent, angelic figures seen in classical works. Rather, these were demonic children, babies with amputated limbs, scarred faces, orphaned children who floated in space, groundless, emanating mysteriously from a blood-streaked background.

Mrs. Carroway looked at the three paintings and was predictably shocked. She surveyed them in horror, her eyes darting from one to the other. Laura glowed with pride as Mrs. Carroway scanned the images, unable to take it all in. But then she noticed that Jeannie Carroway's eyes remained fixed on one painting in particular. It was the grimmest of the three, a depiction of a child enveloped in fire. Sitting in the midst of the inferno, the child's devilish expression lurked behind flames which seemed to emerge from his very soul. Mrs. Carroway could not keep her eyes off of it.

"Do you like that one?" Laura asked, knowing that Jeanie

Carroway's fascination with the painting had nothing to do with like.

"I love it, Laura. I'd like to buy it."

Laura had been waiting all her life to hear those words, had imagined them in dreams, the thought of them pushing her forward through years of struggling. But now that they had been uttered, then and there, coming from Jeannie Carroway who had once worked in the Marketing Department at her mother's office, the words felt empty.

"I don't know," said Laura, unsure of what she could possibly say.

"Oh, please, Laura. You simply must let me have it."

"You see, they kind of go together, and well, someday I'll want to show them all in an exhibition."

"Well then, that's no problem. When you have your exhibition, I'll just lend it to you for as long as you need."

Laura pictured the little card stuck right next to the painting: "Courtesy of Mrs. Jeannie Carroway."

"How much do you want for it?"

Laura immediately thought of the laminated price lists which sat on the smooth wood desks of the galleries in SoHo. She pictured numbers as high as ten thousand, one hundred thousand, numbers which often surprised others, but which to her represented the lifetimes of suffering and sacrifice those artists often endured.

"I'm not sure," said Laura.

"Well, how about three hundred dollars."

Three hundred dollars. It isn't fair, thought Laura. What would she have been offered if this same painting hung against freshly painted white walls, a beautiful gallery owner with slicked back hair and a tight leather skirt pointing at it, expounding on its use of shadow and light? Jeannie Carroway was taking advantage of Laura. Fueled by the squalor of Laura's abode, she would pay as little as she could for a painting which might one day make her a fortune.

Laura looked again at the shiny black fur which enveloped Jeannie Carroway's plump figure, the sharp hairs sticking out of her like the needles of a frightened porcupine. This woman would never have gone near an art gallery, thought Laura. She came to the studio out of curiosity and was unexpectedly overwhelmed. Suddenly, Laura couldn't help feeling a certain tenderness for this old friend of her mother's, the first person to ever offer her money for her art.

"Is that enough?" asked Jeannie Carroway, concerned by Laura's silence.

No, thought Laura, it's not enough. But if she had told Mrs. Carroway the real price of this painting, the woman never would have believed it. "I'm just not sure," said Laura.

"It would look so lovely in my husband's study."

Laura imagined her painting sitting obediently in the Carroway home, doomed never to reach the eyes of a public which might actually recognize its worth, powerless to help propel her into the spotlight. Then she saw all of her paintings, all of her children, sitting in homes across the country, homes of marketing analysts and receptionists and medical supply salesmen, alone and unloved, separated from their natural worlds.

"All right, Jeannie. You can buy it." Laura was tired, tired of fighting and tired of pretending. She would accept who she was and stop waiting around for something which would never come.

Once Jeannie Carroway had taken her painting and left, Laura sat on the couch with her three hundred dollar check and waited eagerly for Henry to come home. As she waited she thought of all the beautiful things she wanted to buy Henry with the money, and soon enough, she became happy with her sale.

Laura and Henry spent days talking about what they'd do with the money, whether to spend it on Burnt Sienna and gold leaf, or new clothes, a new mattress, running shoes, a stereo, a down comforter, or food. There were so many things they needed it seemed impossible to decide. Then Laura suggested they take the entire sum and go out to one of the finest restaurants in New York City for their fifth anniversary. They would order whatever they wanted, a five course meal with the best wine and a fiery desert at the end. For one night, they wouldn't have to feel poor.

Because their anniversary fell on a Friday night, their choice of reservations was limited. They opted for a 6:00 slot rather than waiting until ten at night. Laura wore the black velvet dress she had found at a second hand store two years earlier. It was a designer dress and the saleswoman assured her it was only a year old. Henry wore black pants and a green and blue plaid jacket. He put on a striped tie and Laura was surprised at how well it all matched.

Laura and Henry had heard that even with reservations, they should expect to wait a bit before being seated, this being one of the most popular restaurants in New York City. So they planned to order two glasses of champagne at the bar before dinner. But when they walked in at 6:00 on the dot and told the maitre d' their name, they were promptly shown to their table. It was one of the long row of deuces which lined the huge, frescoed wall, each topped with a flickering yellow flame which made them feel they were entering a church. There were only a few other couples seated in this section of the restaurant and no one sitting directly on Henry and Laura's sides. It felt intimate and private, as if the restaurant had opened early, just for them.

Laura and Henry beamed at each other, proud of their choice of restaurants and happy to have come early, while the restaurant and its employees were still fresh and eager to please.

"Good evening," said the waiter, handing them huge, cream-colored menus.

"Good evening," said Laura, smiling at Henry.

"Can I get you something from the bar?"

"Yes. We'd like to start with two glasses of champagne."

"Very good, sir. Would you like the house champagne?"

"Yes, that will be fine."

The waiter left and Laura and Henry opened the weighty menus. Only Henry's had the prices listed, but neither of them had any intention of noticing what cost what. Both felt completely liberated with the knowledge that they carried three hundred dollars in cash.

"Let's start with the foie gras," said Laura.

"All right. But maybe we should see what the specials are.

What kind of wine should we get?"

"I remember at this restaurant I worked at during college, this guy ordered a Brunello. He had some left over so everybody got to taste. It was amazing."

"Do you remember the year?"

"No."

"That's O.K. Maybe the waiter can recommend one."

The waiter returned with two long flutes of champagne. He set them down in front of Laura and Henry and immediately the two reached for the short, stocky stems. But as they were about to lift the glasses in a toast, the waiter launched into the specials.

"This evening we have a warm goat cheese salad to start, with roasted red peppers, radicchio, and rughetta. Our pasta of the day is a lamb and feta ravioli in a white cream sauce with pine nuts. For our main course we have seared duck with a pear glaze, along with grilled fig on a bed of polenta." The waiter smiled and looked graciously at Laura, then Henry.

"That sounds great," said Henry. The waiter remained.

"We'll just look over the menu a little more if you don't mind," said Laura.

"But of course," said the waiter and quickly walked away.

"So, what do you think?" asked Henry.

"I have to say, the grilled tuna with capers is looking pretty good."

"Mmmm. That does sound good."

"How about you?"

"Actually, I might just get the goat cheese salad and the duck."

"You're always safe with the specials."

Laura and Henry put down their menus and raised their glasses.

"To you, and your first sale," said Henry.

"To us, our fifth anniversary," said Laura.

They clinked their glasses and drank.

Having seen them close their menus, the waiter was quickly at their side.

"And have you decided?"

"Yes," said Henry. "The lady will start with the foie gras and follow with the grilled tuna. I would like the goat cheese salad and the duck."

"Excellent choices, sir. And would you like a bottle of wine with your dinner?"

"Yes. Do you have a nice Brunello?" asked Henry.

"Yes, of course, an excellent one." The waiter collected the menus and headed straight towards the bar.

"You think he'll bring some two hundred year old bottle of wine?" asked Laura.

"Well if he does, we'll just toast its bicentennial."

The hostess brought another couple into the dining room and seated them close to Laura and Henry. The woman was wearing a long black dress, similar to Laura's, but made of a heavy crepe material, the sleeves hanging looser, the waist fitted tighter. Normally, Laura would have congratulated herself for having spent a mere twenty dollars as compared to the two hundred or more dollars this woman must have spent on something similar. But that night, Laura was able to see the finer details of the woman's dress, the subtle way it flowed over her body, the quality of the seams. She suddenly felt uncomfortable against the stiff velvet. The sleeves were too tight and she thought she could feel a stray thread in the neckline.

"Is this what you had in mind, sir?" asked the waiter.

"Yes," said Henry.

The waiter focused all his attention on the careful, precise opening of the bottle of wine. He seemed to have an enormous amount of respect for the bottle, handling it with a crisp white napkin, protecting it from the oiliness of his fingers. As he worked the cork screw gently into the cork, the hostess continued to bring more and more parties into the dining room, until soon there were couples on either side of Henry and Laura.

The cork slipped out easily, with a slight pop when the wine was suddenly reunited with air. The waiter poured a small amount in Henry's glass, allowing him to taste, then proceeded to fill their glasses halfway. He then set the bottle in the middle of the table and looked to his side, noticing for the first time his newly seated customers.

As Henry ate his goat cheese and Laura her foie gras, they watched as their waiter introduced himself to the other couples seated in his station, as he started to attend to their needs, as he smiled at them and made suggestions of what wine to order. Henry wondered if it would ever be the same again between him and the waiter, and he worried that the waiter was spreading himself too thin. In fact, Henry had begun refilling the wine glasses himself, unwilling to wait until the waiter found time to make it back to their table.

"Madame, your grilled tuna. And here, sir, is your seared duck. Enjoy."

Laura and Henry cut into their respective entrées, eyeing one another, anxious to confirm the excellence of their choices.

"The duck is great," said Henry.

"Oh good," said Laura. Meanwhile, she had sliced into her tuna only to find that the one and a half inch thick slab of fish had been left completely raw inside. While Laura was well aware that tuna should always be undercooked, it seemed to her that this fish had not been cooked at all, just simply blackened on the outside, leaving the inside as appetizing as a warm piece of sushi.

"Henry, can you see the waiter?" Laura was facing towards the frescoed wall.

"What's the matter?"

"Oh, I just thought I'd have this cooked a little more."

Henry pursed his lips and lay down his fork, doing his best to hide his exasperation. He waved to the waiter.

"Is anything wrong?"

"Yes," said Henry. "Her fish is undercooked."

"Just a little," said Laura.

"Oh, well, that is how tuna is supposed to be cooked," said the waiter genially.

"I know, it's just that this is, well, practically raw," said Laura.

"Can you just take it back and have them cook it properly?" asked Henry. Laura wished he could have been a little more gentle.

"But of course, sir," and the waiter left with Laura's tuna.

"I'm sorry, Laura."

"Oh no. No big deal."

Henry sat without touching his plate but Laura urged him to continue. "Please, Henry, go ahead, before it gets cold."

"I can wait."

"No, really. You can give me a bite."

So Henry began to eat, offering Laura bites every now and then, which she accepted only once. Minutes passed and Laura kept praying that the waiter would suddenly appear in front of them with her plate of tuna. She wished this less for her own gastronomic pleasure and more so that Henry could finally enjoy his meal. She could tell he was eating with hesitation, wanting to wait until the tuna was returned but not wanting to just sit there while his duck turned cold. He knew that would make Laura unhappy.

Laura stared at the tiny lump of polenta with two halves of a grilled fig lying on top. She watched as Henry ate it in small mouthfuls, cutting the tiny fig into still tinier squares. She wondered why they couldn't have given Henry a bigger portion of polenta. Certainly it was one of the more inexpensive foods and it would have helped to fill him up. As it was, Laura wondered if this dainty portion could possibly satisfy a man of Henry's stature.

"Please, Laura, have some more."

"No, no. I'm fine. He'll be back soon."

And finally, there he was. The waiter had returned with Laura's plate, the tuna having been rearranged to look just like new.

"Thank you," said Laura.

"Of course," said the waiter.

Laura cut into the fish and found it to be cooked through and through. No longer was there even one single patch of translucent red in the entire fillet.

"How is it?"

"Fine," smiled Laura.

Laura took a bite of the fish, its flesh tender and juicy, but not melting in her mouth as she knew it should. She imagined the cook, angry at having his work of art sent back to him, overcooking the fish simply to spite her for her arrogance.

It was time for dessert and as Laura and Henry perused their menus, so much smaller and lighter than the first ones, they noticed the couple next to them receiving their appetizers. That couple's meal was just beginning, thought Laura, appetizers still to be eaten, an almost full bottle of wine. They had everything to look forward to.

"And what can I get you for dessert?" asked the waiter.

"We'll have one crème brulée and one gooseberry tart," said Henry.

"Yes, sir," said the waiter. Somehow he knew that complimenting Henry's choices was no longer necessary.

Laura and Henry clutched the stems of their wine glasses as if someone might take them away. Only one or two sips more, and the Brunello would be finished. Henry raised his hand to Laura's cheek and touched her lightly. He smiled at her. And with his eyes, which glistened moist in the candlelight, he assured her there would still be more to come.

After dessert and liqueurs, the bill was brought in a heavy, leather-bound folder and set down next to Henry. When Henry opened the folder, he found that the bill totaled three hundred and twenty dollars, not including the tip. He looked up at Laura.

"It's over three hundred, isn't it," said Laura.

Henry nodded.

Laura opened her wallet and slipped out her Visa card. "Here, try this." They both knew they had reached their limit months ago, but they figured it was worth a try.

When the waiter came back and set the folder back down without a word, Laura and Henry felt both relief and disappointment. There was something a little unsatisfying about not being caught.

"Thank you very much," said the waiter and smiled his farewell. Laura did her best to smile back, but the waiter had already gone.

They walked out onto the street and the cold night air took them by surprise. Laura quickly wrapped her scarf around her neck and Henry took her arm. It was still only eight o'clock.

"You want to get a cab?" asked Henry.

"Let's just walk," said Laura.

Walking down Fifth Avenue, along Central Park, Henry could still feel his wallet heavy in his back pocket. He began to think again of all that he could buy with such a lot of money. And yet the money was already spent. While he could still feel it, the great bulk of it, it was only just an illusion.

If there was one place in all of New York which Henry would have liked to avoid at that moment, it was this corner, at 59th and Fifth Avenue, where the magnificent Plaza Hotel sat stately and grand. The endless row of horse carriages which ran along the edge of the park seemed to be waiting there for the royalty which was sure to emerge from the palatial hotel. Henry watched Laura as her eyes filled with the vision, and he wanted to cover them, to spare her somehow. They both knew that inside, elegant bedrooms, bathrooms, tearooms, and steam rooms lay hidden from their view, a whole world blocked off by a militant baroque façade.

For one night they had wanted to be a part of all this. With their money, with three hundred dollars, they would buy a place in this world for just one night. But not even this world, this world which went to not just the highest bidder, but any bidder at all, would have them.

They continued to walk, past Murray Hill, the East Village, until they came to their own neighborhood. But even after seven years, they could never have called it home.

They walked up the steps which led to the front door, and inside the first floor window, they saw their neighbors still sitting at the dining room table, eating their Shabbat meal. Laura watched as the family heaped spoonfuls of unidentifiable stews and casseroles onto their plates, drinking thick sweet wine from silver goblets, fighting with each other and laughing and talking about the day's events. How easy it is for these people, thought Laura, knowing their place, where they belong.

"Laura," said Henry.

"What?" said Laura, turning from the window to face Henry who was still standing at the door.

"I forgot the keys," he said.

Laura felt herself go limp. She walked to the edge of the step and sat down.

Henry came and sat down next to her and said, "I'm so sorry, Laura." He wanted to put his arms around her, but he was afraid she might be angry.

Laura shifted in her dress, feeling it's soft velvet snag against the rough concrete. She wished she could get out of that dress. She had wanted to just lie down on her bed and let the fullness in her stomach slowly digest until there were no more remnants of the evening left. But now they would have to wait for a locksmith to come. They would be forced to explain to him what happened, to prove that they were the rightful occupants of their own home.

Laura looked up at Henry whose eyes had turned shiny and sad.

"I'm so sorry," he said again.

Laura put her arms around Henry and squeezed him hard, trying to somehow tell him that it wasn't his fault.

"We could knock on the neighbors' window," said Henry. "Then I could try and pick our lock."

But Laura didn't respond. She just kept squeezing Henry tighter, burying her face in his worn plaid jacket. She didn't want to ask the neighbors to let them in. She didn't want to ask them for anything. Then she realized that she didn't care if she ever stepped foot in that apartment again. She was tired of forcing herself into places that didn't seem to want her at all.

"Let's just stay out here for a while," she said.

And for a moment, Laura felt right with where she was. And she hung on to Henry as tight as she could, trying to make him feel the same.

EURODISNEY

WHEN I FIRST STEPPED INTO THE CENTER OF Florence and saw all those green, red, and white candy-striped façades, I thought I was in Disneyland. The Uffizi didn't help to change this impression, with Botticelli's "The Birth of Venus" looking like some kind of marine life Cinderella, a blond-haired babe with cartoonish blue eyes. This is the real EuroDisney, I thought, with labyrinthian coiled lines full of screaming kids and discontented adolescents, waiting to get on the "David" ride, maybe see the broken toe that some maniac mauled because he was jealous of Michelangelo. Why should high art be spared the violent bursts of the modern age? It was just a matter of time before people ventured out of McDonald's and took their sawed-off machine guns and hatchets into cream-colored museums. Even psychopaths know the real satisfaction isn't in killing seventeen hamburger-eating Texans, but in maiming a piece of the world's posterity.

Now, don't get me wrong. I've got no gripes with the Botticellis, Brunelleschis, or Michelangelos. But I knew there had to be more behind all those Mickey Mouse colors and rock concert crowds. You see, this was my last chance. I had just sold my house in St. Louis, quit my job, left my girlfriend, all so I could move here, to Florence. There simply had to be something more.

I've got a place on Via San Zanobi, and with the word "San" in the name, I'm figuring this Zanobi guy must have been some sort of saint. Every morning I go to the bar next door for breakfast. Now don't jump to any conclusions here because a "bar" in Italy isn't just serving beer and booze, although most of them do have a nice selection of such alcoholic beverages. In Italy, a bar is more like a café. So I walk into my bar—everybody's got his own bar—and right when the counter boy sees me he takes one of these ham and cheese sandwiches and throws it on the little toaster grill. At first I thought it was weird to be having a ham and cheese sandwich for breakfast, but once I saw some old Florentine do it, I figured it was O.K. While we wait for the sandwich to heat up, the boy starts squeezing my blood oranges, until the tall glass is full of the red pulpy liquid. He slides it over to me without a word and hands me my crisped round bread wrapped in tissue. I eye those flecks of rosemary before taking a bite. Just a few sprigs of the stuff. Despite what people think, Italians know there can be too much of a good thing.

This kid's been working here for just one month and he already knows me, knows what I want at eleven o'clock in the morning. Just like the kid before him and the kid before that. It didn't take them long. After two years I've started to become a fixture around here and I haven't decided yet if that's romantic or depressing. I consider telling the poor kid I want something different. Maybe one of those crazy triangle shaped sandwiches made of good old American white bread and filled with a mayonnaisey salad of tuna or mushroom. But I can't seem to tear myself away from this soft oily bread, the aged ham and the smooth tangy cheese, which surely would laugh at their processed American counterparts.

At about noon I go lugging my equipment to one of the more popular piazzas and set up shop. I've got my paints, brushes, and canvases all set up, with a half finished painting sitting on my big old easel. So I guess you could call me an artist and I guess I wouldn't mind if you did. But I know what I am and I'm certainly no artist. I just paint what I see and the similarity is good enough for these tourists who all think I'm Italian because of my thick, wavy, black hair streaked with grey and my big brown eyes. I speak as little as possible so as not to destroy their illusions, and when I do, I just add a nice "uh" to the end of each word. "That'lluh beuh twentyuh dollarsuh." They all just smile and think they're bringing home a real work of Italian art to their aunts in Wilmington.

Artist was not my first choice of careers for my new life in Florence, but what else could a forty-two-year-old insurance salesman from St. Louis hope to do? Bus tables at a restaurant? Teach English? I was very conscious of not emulating my much younger American peers who come to this city to study or hang out for months at a time. They can do whatever they want and get away with it. But I knew that a guy of my age had better reach a certain level of artsiness to justify living in the cradle of the Renaissance. If I didn't, I thought everyone might just get together and send me on home.

I work throughout the three-hour lunch break, when the tourists wander aimlessly around the streets and piazzas. They peer into the closed stores, check the front doors of churches and museums for their hours, looking lost and tired and in need of home, but not wanting to trek back to their tiny hotel rooms where the air is sour and the hotel managers are mean. I stay for them, because this is when they are most in need of something to buy, something to justify their long journey across the Atlantic, to a place where the best pasta seems out of reach, and the neon and smog compete all too well with patinated bronze doors and chipped marble statues.

But once five o'clock rolls around, when the bright Mediterranean sun has dimmed and the Florentine tourism business has mellowed, I am free. At that time, I walk to the front of Santa Maria Novella, its fairy tale façade making me feel like I'm entering the Enchanted Castle. Once I step into the hollow, dark church, a strange reality sets in, a reality so much more mysterious than the brightly hued magic outside. Emerging from one of the barren, grey walls is a faded fresco, the dull pinks and reds barely visible, like the rouge of a tasteful call girl. I stand back, lean forward, searching for an angle which will allow me to discern the look of numbed sorrow on Mary's face, or the Christ figure's brave resignation as he rests, nailed to his cross. While packs of tourists drop coins into boxes, waiting for the artificial lights to illuminate the already glowing paintings which line the walls of the transept, I remain in that dimly lit corner, anxious to keep my find a secret.

When the priests in long black robes start kicking me out around seven o'clock, I head off toward the Arno, to hang out at the Art Bar. Now the Art Bar is a real bar, no ham and cheese, just plenty of booze and all kinds of wines they'll serve by the glass. I drink the house white until around ten, switch to a nice red if I go to dinner, then back to the bar for a glass of scotch.

My friend Piero's over in the corner talking to some American girl. I can tell she's getting tired of him so I prepare myself to take her place when she leaves.

"Bernardo!" he calls. My name is Bernard. At home they called me Bernie, but I think I prefer this Bernardo stuff. Piero's waving me over, even though the American girl is still sitting there. He must have this one pegged for me.

"*Vieni qua, Professore!*" Piero likes to call me Professore. I still haven't figured out if this is supposed to be a sign of respect or derision.

"Have a seat, Bernardo. This is Lola."

"Linda," says Linda.

"My sister's name is Linda," I say and I shake Linda's hand.

"Bernardo, Lola's here studying art," says Piero.

I turn to Linda and say in a low voice, "Don't worry about it. My real name is Bernie."

"Bernardo here is a real live painter, Lola."

"What do you paint?" asks Linda.

"Mostly just churches and stuff. You know, for the tourists."

"Oh," says Linda.

"Lola was just telling me that she hasn't yet seen Masaccio's Cappella Brancacci!"

"I just haven't had a chance yet."

"Oh, Bernardo, you must take her there tomorrow."

Linda's voice begins to flutter, "That's O.K., I . . . "

"Actually, Piero, I'm busy tomorrow." I smile reassuringly at Linda.

"You silly Americans. Such a shame." Piero can barely look at us he's so disgusted.

"I should get going," says Linda, getting up. I get up too, but Piero just sits there, slumped in his chair.

"Nice to meet you, Linda," I say, pronouncing the name long and loud.

"*Arrivaderci*, Lola," says Piero, sad, as if he were bidding adieu to his homeland.

Once Linda's gone I say, "It's your own fault, Piero. You frighten them off."

"Let them be frightened then. I can't waste my time. What did you paint today, Professore?"

"Nothing."

"Nothing?"

"I've still got a lot of inventory to clear."

"Inventory to clear? You sound like a car dealer. And what if Picasso had just stopped at his blue period simply because he couldn't clear his inventory?"

"Is it an Italian phenomenon or is it just you, Piero, who likes to encourage the talentless with such blind faith?"

"I'm afraid it's a long tradition in our culture, Bernardo. We know the great artists will get their glory after they're dead, so why not give the mediocre ones a good time while they're still alive?"

"I appreciate that."

"You need a rich, old woman to patronize you."

"No, actually, that's the last thing I need."

"Then you could stop painting those silly churches and do some real work."

"I like painting those silly churches."

"Oh, it's absurd. All you are is a very expensive camera!"

Usually Piero will wait at least three or four drinks before he starts calling me an expensive camera, but it seems things have been accelerated this evening by our unexpected visitor. I suggest we go out for an early dinner.

"All right, but I want to go to the Chinese restaurant."

"Oh, Piero, please."

"Come."

The next day, after work, I go to the church of the Carmine to see Masaccio's Brancacci Chapel. As I maneuver through the cars which flank the church's entrance, I wonder how it might have been if I'd brought Linda here.

We'd have walked across one of the bridges, maybe the Ponte Vecchio, over to the other side of the Arno, where Florence seems to have calmed its constant need to please and just goes on about its business as if the town across the river was just a showy neighbor. We'd have stopped in at the little café near the church and had a cream-filled cornetto and a cappuccino, while the barmen watched soccer on their portable black-and-white TV. Then I'd have led her into the church, perhaps taking her hand, and brought her to my favorite panel.

For minutes we'd have stared at the fresco in silence, the one where Adam and Eve are expelled from the Garden of Eden. She, like me, would never have seen such a forceful depiction of that hideous event. We'd have looked into Eve's dark sunken eyes, into the deep cavern of her gaping mouth, almost hearing her strangled moan. And Adam would have been next to her, covering his face in shame, his magnificent body hunched into a disgrace from which he would never recover. We'd have looked at these first mortals, covering their genitals, wailing like children as they leave their world of perfection and angels and enter a new world of falsity and vice. Right there Linda and I would have had a sudden urge to embrace, to bury our heads in each others shoulders, to clutch one another in terror. But instead, we would have squeezed each other's hands, assuring one another that we'd be alone soon enough.

I decide that I'm quite glad not to be here with Linda. I didn't come all the way to Florence to fool around with some twenty-year-old American girl. What was I thinking? I walk through the church, looking at the other people out of the corner of my eye, anxious that I might see Linda at any moment. I see the back of a woman with long dark hair lighting a candle, and I think, maybe that's her. Even though I know this woman is not Linda, or even Lola for that matter, I keep looking.

Sometimes you forget that there are people who actually come into these churches to pray. It seems that is exactly what this woman is doing, praying. She must be Italian, I think. She's got long thin legs wrapped in brown nylon, a short skirt, and a pale beige leather jacket. Her long dark hair hangs heavy down her back, curling effortlessly.

She turns around and I see her face, pale olive skin and dark, wide eyes. So Italian is this young woman, thin and starved, eager to marry so she can finally get some nourishment. I want to take her and feed her, assure her that her beauty need not be compromised. She sees me, sees me staring, and luckily, smiles. I quickly turn back to the fresco before her smile turns to a frown. Suddenly, my Eve is too tragic for me to bear and I rush toward the light of the doorway.

I practically throw myself out the door, bounding down the steps into the car lot, and from the corner of my eye I can see the beige and brown blur of her. I feel with all my might her black-eyed stare upon me, so I turn to face her. She's looking at me all right, still smiling, as if the smile from moments before never had a chance to die down. I smile back.

"*Hai fretta?*" she says. She's asking if I'm in some sort of hurry, but I don't detect any sarcasm in the question, just an oddly sincere curiosity.

"*No, non ho fretta. Solo un po di paura.*" No hurry, I say, just a little fear. No one has to tell me that sometimes the most blatant admission of weakness is what truly makes a man appear strong.

"You are English?" she asks. I guess the strength of my accent supersedes everything else.

"American," I say, hoping this woman favors the dynamism of the Americas to England's good grammar.

"America," she says, clearly pleased. "I've been to America twice."

"Which part?"

"New York and California," she says. "But why are you afraid?"

"Oh, I guess it must have been Eve in there."

"Eve?"

"You know, Adam and Eve. Eva."

"Ah, Eva. Yes. She is very fearful."

"Frightful," I say.

"Yes," she says. The longer it stays silent like this, the more time we both have to contemplate the awkwardness of our little duo. I begin to feel my grey waves going limp against my skull, while her eyes start wandering off into the piazza in front of us, as if she's waiting for an old blue Vespa to pick her up and bring her to the nearest make-out spot.

"You like Masaccio?" I decide not to give up so easily.

"Yes, I think so."

"Think so?"

"I only know him in this church," she says humbly.

"Well, I think that's quite enough," I say, and her eyes beam with pride.

Now she's looking at her feet, maybe because she doesn't want to discourage me by looking too far beyond the steps of the church.

"Are you waiting for someone?" I ask.

"No," she says quickly.

"Maybe I could walk you home then."

"Thank you. Yes, I will like that."

We walk through the shaded streets, unsure if the sun behind these ancient buildings is falling down towards the horizon, screaming its last rays of yellow light, or if it has already fallen, the reds and oranges bleeding into the now empty sky.

I can't remember having walked down the streets of Florence like this before, more interested in the person walking next to me than the doorways or the cafés I am passing. I realize I don't even know her name.

"What is your name?"

"Margherita."

At that moment, I'm sure this woman will never disappoint me.

"And what are you called?" she asks.

"Bernardo," I say.

We're walking in silence but it doesn't seem to matter. The pleasant click of her brown leather shoes against the cobblestones is enough. I begin to worry that any minute she'll stop in front of an entryway and announce "We're here."

We pass a wine shop I've been to before. The walls are lined with wines and bottles of grappa while in the back are a couple of wooden tables.

"Would you like something to drink?" I ask, stopping in front of the wine bar.

She looks at me, as if this might be one of the more important decisions of her life. She looks inside the bar, then at the street in front and then at me again.

"Yes. O.K."

We sit at the smaller of the two tables, the one stuck in the corner, and both of us order a glass of white wine. I ask the old man to bring us a plate of his special bruschetta as well.

"You are an artist," she says to me.

"Yes, I am," I reply. "How did you know?"

She reaches out and touches the breast pocket of my white cotton shirt. I look down and notice a spot of green paint. Her hand moves up to my hair. She does not push a few strands back behind my ear as her slender fingers with their painted nails seem to promise. Instead, she grabs a handful and tugs gently.

"You have very nice hair," she says and lets go.

"It's practically all grey," I say. I can't hide the pain I feel at watching my smooth, jet black hair wither into bristly strands of wire.

"You worry about getting old?" she asks, concerned, even surprised.

"Not worry, really. I just don't like some of the effects I guess."

"Men do not need to worry," says Margherita. "Women must worry."

She looks too sad for such a generic statement, and yet there she is, the corners of her terra cotta mouth turned down, her sparkling black eyes gazing off to the side. Before I can reach out, touch her hand, comfort her, the old man comes with our wine and bruschetta.

"How old are you, Margherita?"

"Twenty-six."

I look down and smile. I pick up a piece of the toast covered with truffles and offer it to her.

"You've never been here before?" I ask.

"No," she says. She's probably been to very few of the establishments scattered throughout her neighborhood. Italian mothers don't allow their children to stray far from the family kitchen.

"You live with your family," I say.

"Yes."

I take a bite of my bruschetta, a sip of the wine. But my contentment is suddenly halted by the look of quiet distress on Margherita's face.

"What's wrong?" I ask her.

She smiles and takes a sip of her wine, as if to prove to me it's nothing. She reaches for my hand and squeezes it.

"Nothing," she says. "I'm just happy to be here."

The sky is a deep blue when we finally leave the wine bar. We stand outside the doorway, in the middle of the empty street.

"Shall I take you home?"

Margherita stands for a moment in silence, looking, I believe, towards her family's apartment. "No," she says. "No, take me somewhere else."

We walk across the bridge, wide and plain and open, avoiding the chaos of the Ponte Vecchio which seems to be paved in gold watches and diamond necklaces. When we finally reach my front door, Margherita stops.

"You have your own apartment?" she asks.

"Yes, of course."

She looks up at the building, as if it would somehow assure her. Once I actually open the door with my very own key, she's convinced.

Inside I quickly turn on lights. I clear a place for her on the sofa, throwing paint soaked rags and old canvases into the bedroom.

"It's O.K. It's nice in here," she says.

"Well, I usually keep it cleaner."

She takes off her jacket and sits down on the sofa.

"Can I get you something to drink?" I ask.

"No," she says. "Come here and sit down."

I sit down and we just look at each other in silence, our sides pressed against the back of the sofa, our arms stretched across the back cushion.

"I feel fortunate to meet you," she says.

"I do, too."

"I am glad I went to the church early today. Usually I go later."

"You go to church everyday? To pray?"

"In this period, yes."

"Can I ask why?"

Margherita clutches my arm. "No, I don't want to talk about it now."

"O.K.," I say.

She lets go of my arm and moves closer to me. It's closer than she's been all evening and I can see things I hadn't seen before. I can see the smoothness of her skin, dark and taut against her jaw. Her lips, the color faded, rough and pink. She leans over and kisses me on the mouth and I respond by leaning towards her, putting my arms around her waist, my hands resting on her lower back. I lean further, over her, lifting and lowering her underneath me. I lie down on top of her, kissing her. I worry I am hurting her, that I am too heavy. But she gives me no sign of discomfort, responding eagerly to my kisses, resting her hands gently on my shoulders.

We stay on the sofa like that for over an hour, then finally move to my bedroom. When I remove her clothes, I remember that I haven't been with anyone like this since I left America, not for two whole years. I stare at her nakedness in amazement, her youthful body still proud of its own deficiencies. She undresses me, pressing her body against mine. While we stand there, I feel cold and large, until finally we lie down on the bed and I become weightless, free to wrap myself around her warm brown body, to soak her of her energy which she gives freely.

At around ten o'clock she gets out of bed and begins dressing.

"You're leaving?" I ask.

"Yes, I must."

"Why?"

"They will worry."

"You can call."

"No, really, it's better that I leave."

"Can I have your phone number?"

"No, you must not call me at home. I can call you."

I get out of bed and slip on my shorts. I go to my desk and scribble out my phone number.

"Here," I say. "You'll call me soon I hope."

"Tomorrow," she says, then kisses me good-bye.

It's still early so I decide to go to the Art Bar for a drink.

As soon as I walk in I see Linda at the bar, talking and laughing with a middle-aged Italian man. There she is in her faded jeans and an old suede jacket which she must have bought in the used section of the market. Her green backpack hangs off her shoulder and her straight brown hair is tied back in a ponytail. She's got a pint of beer in her hand which she sips every so often, never taking her eyes off the man who speaks to her in Italian. I wonder if she really knows what he's saying.

Linda sees me and gives me a big friendly wave as if we were old pals.

"Hi there," she says, grinning, trying to look at the Italian guy and me at the same time.

"Hi," I say.

"*Sandro, questo e Bernie. Bernie, Sandro,*" says Linda, her rolling 'r's,' sounding like she has some sort of sinus infection.

"*Piacere,*" I say, shaking Sandro's hand. He just nods and smiles, eager for me to leave.

"Your friend Piero's back there," she says to me. "He's a strange one."

"Yeah," I say, but really I'm annoyed that she thinks just because we're both Americans, she can bad mouth my Italian friend. I start to move away.

"See you later," she says with excessive enthusiasm. Maybe she's trying to make Sandro think that she's got a lot of friends here.

"Yeah, see you later." I walk away from Linda as if I'm walking

32

away from an entire lifetime. I can't believe I ever considered spending an afternoon with her, considered sharing with her Masaccio's Adam and Eve. Linda is everything I had wanted to get away from when I left America. She's downtown St. Louis and the neighborhood strip mall and the office receptionist and my sister. No wonder Piero had tried so desperately to rename her Lola.

I practically run to the corner where Piero sits and he welcomes me with open arms.

"Professore! Where have you been?"

"I told you I was busy this evening."

"Did you see your friend at the bar with that awful Sandro?"

"Yes I did."

"If you were any sort of real man you would rescue her immediately."

"Sorry, Piero. I think there may be someone else who needs rescuing."

"What do you mean?"

"I've met a woman."

"Who?"

"Margherita."

"Oh no! Bernardo! What have you done?"

"What? I just met her a few hours ago. What's wrong?"

"She's Italian!"

"Well, most women in Italy are."

"What about Lola? She's not Italian."

"Enough with Lola, already! Don't you see? She's not even Lola, she's Linda! Plain old, pitiful Linda who comes to Florence for a few months, fools around with every Tom, Dick, and Sandro she can get her hands on, then goes back to her depressing little American town to lead the rest of her depressing little American life!"

Piero sits silently, staring at his drink. I decide to just go on up to the bar if a waiter doesn't come pretty soon to take my order.

"Margherita, I guess, is very beautiful?"

"Yes."

"Young?"

"Twenty-six."

"Listen, Bernardo. I don't mean to discourage you. You of course should follow your heart. But I know Italian women better than you."

"And I know American women better than you."

"This is true," says Piero. "I guess I just prefer your Lindas and Lauras and Marys. Their baggy clothes and pale faces. They seem so much more real."

"Well, Margherita is real, too, without the baggy clothes."

"Then I am truly happy for you, my friend."

The next day I work at home on some new canvases, waiting for Margherita's call. At around four o'clock the phone rings.

"*Pronto.*"

"Bernardo?"

"Yes."

"It's me, Margherita."

"Hello."

"I call to see if you would like to meet."

"Yes, very much. Would you like to come to my place?"

"Let us meet outside somewhere first."

"The wine bar, near the church?"

"No, no. Somewhere near you."

"There's a bar next door."

"O.K. I meet you there at six."

I can tell the boys behind the bar are surprised when Margherita enters and walks straight over to my table. I have never brought anyone in here before.

I watch as Margherita approaches, dressed this evening in brick red and black, and I feel like the entire Italian peninsula is walking towards me. Everything else had just been mere elements, the food, the art, the bars, Piero. But here is all of Italy personified in one single entity, with her earth tones and elegance, understated and sublime. Margherita was what lay behind all the glitter.

"*Ciao,*" she says and kisses each cheek with the ease of a close friend.

"I hope this place is O.K.," I say, suddenly aware of the yellow plastic chairs and the stained red tablecloths.

"It is perfect."

"Why didn't you want to meet at my place?" I ask.

"I wanted for us to talk first," she says smiling and I take this to mean it would be all right for me to hold her hand.

"I waited all day for your call," I say, alarmingly unashamed.

"I'm sorry," she says.

"Why must you be so secretive?"

"You live alone, Bernardo. You don't have to worry about keeping things private."

"So you want to keep me private?"

"Yes, secret, all to myself," and she squeezes my hand.

"Is it because of my age?" I say.

"Of course not! I do not care how old you are."

"But I imagine your parents wouldn't be so happy to know you're seeing a forty-two-year-old artist from America."

"I do not know what they would feel."

"I'm not exactly an ideal prospect for a husband."

"I am not looking for a husband."

"You're not interested in marriage?"

"Must we talk about such things?"

"Of course not."

"Look, Bernardo, I'm interested in love, in passion, in being with a man . . . like you. Marriage is something else."

"I could easily sacrifice marriage for love and passion." I lean over and kiss her and she kisses me back.

We sit for a moment in silence, Margherita looking down at the stained red tablecloth.

"I am engaged to be married," she says.

"You mean, you *were* engaged to be married?"

"No, I am. Now."

Ideas begin to pop into my head, but I shoot them down, one by one, like a cowboy overturning a neat row of old tin cans. Only now do I realize how much I really want from this woman.

"To whom?"

"A boy I know for many years. Our families are close friends."

"I see."

"I do care for him very much, Bernardo. I can't imagine not having him in my life. I just don't feel . . . passion for him. You understand?"

"Yes."

"I need something more."

"Like me."

"Yes."

"Look, Margherita, I'm happy to give you what you're looking for, I just don't know how I feel about breaking up your engagement."

"But I don't want to break up my engagement."

"I'm sorry, I don't understand."

"I must marry him, Bernardo. I'm twenty-six years old. His family is giving us an apartment. Right on the Arno."

"And from me you'll get your passion."

"Yes, from you I will get what is truly important."

Margherita is squirming around in her seat, waiting for my reply. There she is slipping and sliding around in that yellow plastic cup of a chair, like she's on some sort of amusement park ride. And I feel like one of those unshaven men in maroon corduroys and a hooded sweatshirt, manning the controls down below. I don't feel much like letting her off.

"Bernardo," she says, her long lashes blinking, her mouth puckering.

All of a sudden, Margherita doesn't look so out of place here, against the yellow plastic and the bright red polyester. Maybe those boys behind the bar knew it all along.

"Bernardo?"

I've always been curious about the relationship between the brain and the senses. Smell, taste, vision, it all goes back to the brain. The brain is what makes one person see beauty and another see ugliness. And once new information is inserted into the brain, the vision changes accordingly. Thus, what was once beautiful suddenly becomes ugly.

Anybody with any sort of real brain looks beyond the surface for his dose of beauty. Between the cracks, amidst the shadows, whatever lies most out of reach.

THE COOKER LADY

FIVE IN THE MORNING AND JOANIE'S UP, trying out her recipes for the afternoon show. Flour's flying onto her neatly arranged piles of nutmeg and cinnamon, an unexpected snowstorm over a condiment tundra. She still has to make the kids' lunches, although why they can't just buy them at school on Fridays she'll never understand.

"Buy their lunches?" her husband chimes in. "What a waste! Can't imagine there's a lot of nutritional value in that slop. What're they still counting ketchup as a vegetable? Heh, heh." Her husband has no qualms about resuscitating a lifeless joke at her expense.

Bologna on white bread, they'll like that. Where's the mayonnaise? Any other day Joanie would have yanked out the food processor and from the unlikely union of egg and oil, whipped up her own, but instead she just slaps slices of compressed blood and guts onto half-baked lard and lets the rest slide. They'll hate her when they bite into their pristine triangles, mouths watering, expecting a flood of oily white goo to ooze out and slip down their throats, only to find a dry paste stuck to the backs of their teeth. They'll forget by half-past three when they come home and stick fishsticks in the toaster oven.

"I'm bringing some clients over for dinner tonight," says her husband. Clients. Where are all these clients coming from? She wonders if her husband isn't just soliciting people off the street.

"How many?" asks Joanie.

"Four," answers her husband.

When the hell is she supposed to prepare dinner for all these clients? She'll be at the show most of the day and by the time she gets home she'll be too exhausted to worry about serving dinner to clients. Maybe she could serve them the food from the show. She'll just heat it up, nobody thinking for a moment that the food had been sitting in a stuffy studio under hot lights, the steely soot of camera equipment, wire cables, and gaffer's tape transposing itself onto its surface.

"Will you be here when we get home?" asks her daughter.

"No, honey. Remember to take your key."

"Mom, are we latchkey children?" asks her son.

Latchkey children. Her husband looks up at her, waiting for a response, but she won't give him the satisfaction. She's been home to greet her children from school, her husband from work, every day for the last fifteen years.

"It's only on Fridays, dear," says Joanie.

"Joanie! Where've you been?" asks the producer, handing off her clipboard to an assistant with an Olympic-relay urgency.

Joanie looks at her watch. 1:30. Right on time. "I got stuck in traffic, sorry."

"C'mon, we've got to get you to make-up."

"Make-up?" Joanie hadn't worn it last week, her debut.

"Yes, Joanie. Bill's worried you're looking a little peaked." Joanie touches her face, as if her fingers can somehow sense her wan complexion.

"Just sit still." The make-up man is applying a thin mauve line along Joanie's upper lip. She wonders if the industrial size container of light blue eye shadow is intended for her or reserved only for the occasional visits from the local theater troupe.

38

"Joanie!" she hears in the distance. A second later and the producer is standing over her, the director at her side.

"I told you, Bill. Gerard is fixing her right up."

"Good." They talk as if Joanie were under a general anaesthetic, being operated on by an inexperienced but talented young resident.

"How you doing there, Joanie?" Now she's pulling through.

"Fine," says Joanie to the director.

"You gonna do as well as last week?" asks the director.

"You bet," answers Joanie and she gives him the smile which they all seem to love.

"That's what I wanna hear." The director smiles back. He takes the producer by the arm and they walk away, speaking to each other in whispers.

The make-up man puts down his brush, straightens Joanie's shoulders and looks at her in the mirror. "You're a star!" he says.

"So look out for that cold front," says the weatherman. "It should spell the end of this Native American summer we've been having."

"I guess that means no picnics in the park this weekend," says the anchorwoman.

"Heh, heh, heh, I wouldn't advise it, Mary. But I'm sure everyone will be eating in after seeing what our little cooker lady is concocting over yonder."

"Mmm, you're right there, Ed. It looks wonderful."

"You save me some of that strudel, Joanie!"

A voice is heard off-camera. "You got it, Ed."

"We'll be right back with our own Chef Joan after these messages," the anchorwoman says to the camera.

The red light goes off and it seems as if the entire crew comes pouncing onto Joanie.

"Don't forget to look into the camera, Joanie."

"I think she needs a little more blusher."

"Joan!" says the weatherman, sure that his blue eyes and flaxen hair will draw Joanie's attention away from the others.

"Yes?" answers Joan. She's still trying to get her pastry dough to stop sticking to the counter.

"Your stuff looks great," he says, looking into Joanie's mascaraed eyes.

"Thank you," says Joanie, feeling her lined lips puckering as she says the *yooo*.

"Sixty seconds."

"All right, Joanie. Just keep it natural. That's why we love you."

"Then all you have to do is roll the dough over, carefully, like this . . ." Joanie's lightly floured fingers smooth the fine layer of dough over a spicy mix of dried fruit. "And there you have it." She looks up into the camera and gives her audience a modest but proud grin.

"Joanie, you make it look so easy," says the anchorwoman.

"But it is," says Joanie. She turns to the oven and pulls out a ready-to-eat strudel.

"Now that's what I've been waiting for," says the weatherman.

Joanie begins slicing the strudel into hearty portions, laying them on paper napkins and handing them to her fellow performers.

"Mmm, delicious," says the anchorwoman, stretching her lips over the greasy crust, careful not to smear her lipstick.

"Tell me, Joanie," says the weatherman, his eyebrows furrowed, strudel in hand. "How long have you been cooking professionally?"

"Well, I guess about two weeks now," says Joanie.

The weatherman guffaws and the anchorwoman takes another bite.

"Looks like we've got us an honest to goodness Cinderella story!"

The red light goes off for the last time and Joanie's little kitchen counter suddenly becomes an island oasis in the middle of a grey-blue wasteland. They are coming in hordes, cameramen, assistants, and anchor folks alike. They tear apart the strudel and dig into the chicken platter with grimy fingers, gradually turning their attentions to the caviar-covered torte and the roasted pepper and eggplant salad. Joanie watches as tonight's dinner is ravaged by highly paid employees who act as if they haven't eaten for days. She doesn't care though, in fact she's relishing it. Just seeing her creations in this strange setting is a thrill. Like a fearless exhibitionist flaunting her wares. She watches these strangers devour her food, handling it, stuffing it into their mouths, the juices dripping down their chins.

"Joanie, I want to see you in my office," says the producer.

Joanie steps into the producer's office, large and cluttered, with glass table tops and velvet chairs, the office of an executive too busy for numbered prints and oriental rugs.

"Sit down, Joanie," says the producer.

Joanie sits.

"What are your plans for next week?"

"Plans?"

"What's the menu, for next week's show?"

"Well, I thought I'd focus on a specific fruit. The apple, for example."

"Yes, tell me more."

"It seems to me, that the apple is really one of the most popular fruits, and there's so much you can do with it."

"There you go!" the producer slaps her hand down on the pile of scripts which sit on her desk. The glass shudders.

"Sorry?"

"You're a natural, Joanie. Give the people what they want, that's what you're thinking. Right? Am I right?"

"Yeah."

"Apples. It's so simple. What do people like?"

"Apples."

"Exactly."

"I thought I'd do baked apples, an apple compote, apple butter."

"Steering away from the apple pie."

"Oh yeah, I thought that would be too obvious."

"Good thinking," says the producer.

"Then, if people respond well to that, I could move onto a different fruit—banana, or maybe a vegetable. Potato, zucchini . . ."

"Hold on a minute, Joanie, I gotta get Steve in here."

Alone in the office, Joanie's eyes quickly dart from bookcase to pen set to the row of three televisions built into the wall. She wonders how long she would have to be left sitting there before she'd start rummaging through the producer's drawers. She figures it would have to be a very long time.

"It's just like last week, Rita. The board's lit up like a Christmas tree!" the executive producer says to the producer as they walk back into the office.

"Steve, this is Joanie."

"Joanie," the executive producer holds out his hand to Joanie who takes it with a smile. She says nothing, understanding this is no time for small talk. He turns back to the producer. "I'm telling you, Rita, we gotta move on this."

It's already four o'clock and Joanie's wondering when she'll get out of there so she can start getting dinner ready for tonight. She wishes she had asked which clients were coming because if they're the same ones as last week, she'd better not serve chicken again. And then there's the odd one who doesn't eat meat. She can't really get upset with him since a vegetarian in the real estate business seems somehow holy to Joanie.

"Joanie, we're sending you to New York," says the producer. "We'll put you on the six o'clock flight which will get you there in time for a dinner meeting at Bouley."

Joanie isn't sure which of the previously mentioned words she should repeat with a questioning lilt. New York? Six o'clock flight? Bouley? A second passes and the choice is obsolete.

"You don't know what Waxman's up to, do you, Joanie," says the executive producer.

"Um, no, I . . . who?"

"Ramone Waxman! The Classic Cook! You don't know the Classic Cook?" The executive producer looks at the producer who shrugs her shoulders. Joanie figures New York is off, which will still leave her time for the pasta *al forno* she'd been thinking about for tonight.

"The Classic Cook. I know." Joanie recognizes Waxman's stage name.

"And what do you know, Joanie?" asks the executive producer.

"Well, I know he has a real fondness for ginger."

The executive producer smirks and walks across the room, his back to Joanie.

"Waxman's been a real thorn in the network's side from day one," says the executive producer. "But even so, he soared, higher and faster than anyone else I've seen in this business. There was something about him, what it was, I . . ." the executive producer shakes his head. "He seemed to speak to the people. Directly. As if he'd jumped past the cameras and the lights, right into people's homes. They trusted him. They loved him." He turns around and looks at Joanie. "You, Joanie. I can feel it. It's the same for you." The executive producer turns away, as if he can't bear the site of Joanie any longer, as if her glow would blind him, the glow of a prophet.

"We're in a crisis situation here, Joanie," says the producer. She will lay it all on the line. "The network honchos are going in for the kill and they need a live body to cover their tracks."

"And not just anybody!" the executive producer reels around and looks straight into Joanie's eyes.

"For the past nine months they've been looking, Joanie," continues the producer. "They've issued a mandate. Across the country, from Akron to Albuquerque, local stations have been combing their districts for the right one."

"In New York you'll be meeting with the network heads and their lawyers," says the executive producer, seeming to have regained his composure. "We'll be sending along tapes, but we think the numbers speak for themselves."

"Joanie," says the producer, "we need a yes and we need it now." So calm the producer seems to Joanie. Calm yet firm. Like her mother. Joanie wants to wrap her arms around her.

"I have to call home," says Joanie.

The executive producer and the producer smile, but it fades fast. "You can use my office," says the producer. "We'll be right back."

Joanie walks behind the producer's desk and sits in her black leather chair. She begins dialing home, but after the first three numbers she's lost. Is it seven-four or four-seven? She'd rather not look it up so she gives four-seven a try.

"Hello?"

"Penny?"

"Mom? Where are you?"

"I'm still at the studio, honey."

"Studio?"

"Penny, what are you doing?"

"Making fishsticks."

"O.K., dear, but make sure you turn the oven off when you take them out."

"I will."

"Where's Freddy?"

"I don't know."

"You don't know?"

"I don't know! He must have gone out."

"Out where?"

"Mom!"

"O.K. Just tell him to stay inside when he comes home."

"When are you coming home, Mom?"

"Well, dear, I . . . Penny, check and see if Freddy's in the backyard will you?"

"Oh, Mom! He's probably over at the pond."

"C'mon dear, do it for me."

Joanie waits, the receiver pressing hard against her ear.

"No, he's not there."

"O.K., dear. Now I want you to go eat your fishsticks and stay inside. I'll call you back in a little bit. All right?"

"O.K."

"Bye, honey."

"Bye."

Joanie sits, finger to lip, thinking. Suddenly, a young woman in her twenties wearing black walks in.

"I've got you a 6:10 flight on United," says the assistant. "Are you a frequent flyer?"

"Oh, no," says Joanie.

"Would you prefer a window or an aisle?"

"Aisle, please."

"I'm trying to get you into first class, but they're pretty booked."

"Oh, that's O.K., I . . . "

"I'll do my best."

"Thank you."

The assistant leaves and Joanie picks up the phone and dials.

"Honey?"

"Joanie?"

"It's me."

"What's up?"

"Well, there's a little problem about tonight."

"Oh, Joanie, don't start in. Just make anything. They don't care!"

"No, it's not . . . "

"Shirley, can you get in here? I told you I needed the Conway contract. Listen, Joanie, this is a bad time."

"I called the house and Freddy's not there."

"He's probably out at the pond with the other kids."

"He usually tells me when he's going there."

"Well, Fridays are different, aren't they Joanie?"

Joanie can hear Shirley in the background telling her husband the Conway file is missing.

"I gotta go, Joanie. I'll see you tonight. And don't worry about what to make. I'm sure whatever you do will be fine."

Her husband hangs up.

Joanie hangs up. Her eyes fall to the desktop where papers and files lie in a haphazard pile. On top sits a legal contract with pink florescent lines dashing across bold, black print. Performer. Waxman. Duration of Contract. Seven years. Yearly salary. Two million. As if the paper, the words themselves, caught her in the act, Joanie runs to the other side of the desk and sits in the blue velvet chair.

"Did Lisa get your flight information squared away?" the producer asks as she enters the office.

"Lisa? Oh, yes, Lisa. She did."

"Good." The producer goes to the velvet chair opposite Joanie and sits down. "Look, Joanie, I know all this must seem crazy to you . . . "

"Oh, no."

"All I ask is that you bear with us for a while. It all happened so suddenly, you coming along like this. We don't have time to think, we've got to act."

"I totally understand," says Joanie, smiling at the producer. Joanie wishes she and the producer could sit together in those blue velvet chairs all night. They could drink coffee and talk and when they got hungry, the producer could send her assistant out to get them Chinese food.

Suddenly, the executive producer comes in. "Have you seen this fax from Jim yet, Rita?"

The producer pats Joanie on the hand and rises to meet the executive producer. "No, what is it?"

"He says some station in Salt Lake is sending someone up tonight."

"You've got to be kidding."

"There was talk about having him join the meeting, but Jim nixed that pretty quick."

"Thank God."

"It must be getting around that we're taking a shot. They're desperate. They'll try anything at this point."

"Yeah, well, let 'em try."

"Still . . . " the executive producer looks at Joanie. "I want you to push your weight around up there. Don't let them try and group you with any of those other losers. Remember who you are, Joanie."

Joanie looks at the executive producer closely, waiting for him to say more.

"Would you all mind if I made another phone call?" asks Joanie.

46

The producer and executive producer do not even attempt to hide their annoyance. "Should we leave you alone?"

"Oh no, you can stay right here. It'll only be a second."

Joanie goes to the phone which sits underneath the row of televisions. She turns her back to the producers.

"Hello, Penny?"

"Mom, when are you coming home?"

"Soon, dear. I just have a few more things to take care of."

"I'm bored."

"Hasn't Freddy come back yet?"

"No."

"Oh, dear."

"What's the big deal about him?"

"I just want to know where he is."

"I told you he's probably at the pond."

"Has your father called?"

"No."

"O.K., honey, just stay put and I'll see you soon."

"Bye."

"Bye, bye."

Joanie presses the reset button and dials.

"Hello, Shirley?"

"Yes?"

"Hi, Shirley, it's Joanie."

"Oh, hi."

"Is my husband there?"

"Oh, no, he went out for a drink with the clients."

"Do you know where they went?"

"No, can't say that I do."

"O.K., well thanks, Shirley."

"Sure."

Joanie hangs up. She turns to the producers. "Do you think I could go home now and get ready before my flight?"

The producers step towards her. "Joanie, there's no time for you to go home," says the executive producer.

"What?"

"You'll never make your flight. You'll have to leave from here," says the producer.

"But, I have to. I mean, I really have to go home."

"Joanie, I'm afraid that's impossible," says the executive producer.

"My son, he's not home from school yet."

"He's probably off playing with the other kids."

"But he usually tells me when he's going to be late."

"How could he tell you if you're not at home, Joanie?"

"But . . . "

"Besides, you can call home from the airport. Make sure he's home safe before you ever get on the plane."

"It's just that, well, and my husband is out, and his clients are . . . "

"You can call him from the airport, too."

"I don't know . . . "

"Joanie, we have no other choice. You miss that flight and we'll all miss our chance."

Joanie looks hard at the producer and executive producer. They seem to Joanie so sincere. They're thinking about me, aren't they, thinks Joanie. They're thinking about my best interests. She looks at the producer, an attractive woman of thirty-five, younger than Joanie—but that smile, that concerned, motherly smile. And the executive producer, giving her fatherly advice, telling her to throw her weight around.

"I'm sorry," says Joanie, "I have to go home. I'll go as fast as I can. I can make the flight. I know I can make it."

Traffic's light and Joanie makes it home in only fifteen minutes.

"Mom!"

"Hi, honey! Is Freddy back yet?"

"No."

"Oh, Penny. Where could he be?"

"Mom, the good frogs don't even come out till after dark."

"I'm going to go wash up, honey."

"Stay and play with me, Mom!"

"I'm sorry, dear, I'm in a big hurry."

*

Joanie stands motionless under the scalding hot water, water which would scorch anyone else, but not Joanie, whose face has hovered over steaming casseroles, whose arms have been sprayed with the spurting outshoots of boiling soups, whose hands have gripped the fiery handles of cast iron pans. She holds her head down, letting the water glide down her body from every angle. Down her back, her arms, her chest, in her ears flows the water, creating the sounds of ringing and knocking and buzzing. Joanie stands still, waiting, wondering if any of those sounds could be Freddy coming home.

She stands naked in front of the full-length mirror which hangs on the door of the bathroom. She pours a pool of thick beige cream into her cupped palm and begins smoothing it over her legs. Suddenly, her dull, chapped skin turns golden and shiny as a well-basted turkey. She covers her entire body with the per-fume-scented cream and then wraps herself in a thick white towel.

Her silky panty hose slide effortlessly up her legs, fitting snugly around her hips and her protruding stomach. She reaches to the other side of the bed and takes a tan colored camisole which she slips over her head. She steps into her walk-in closet and takes a heavy gabardine suit from the back. She pulls on the skirt which fastens easily, and then puts on the jacket whose satin lining lies flat over the thin camisole.

The hallway is dark. She walks down the staircase carefully and enters the living room. The evening sky is still a rich royal blue, but there is not enough light passing through the huge win-dows to illuminate the quiet room. She goes to the bar and pours herself a drink. Plain scotch she pours. She drinks without ice, not wanting to enter the brightly lit kitchen.

She sits on the sofa and leans back slowly, slightly conscious of not wrinkling her suit. She is silent, breathing softly, listening. Far away, from the other end of the house, she can barely hear the flat drone of the television. In the dark she sits and stares, out the win-dows which line the room, watching the blue of the sky slowly turn to black.

MYANMAR

THE SUN SHINES HARD ON THEIR DILATED EYES, and they feel like vampires, entering a shocking world of light without shadow. Such disorientation after only two hours in the dark of a movie theater? But how far they've traveled! Over oceans, across fields, backwards in time to a place requiring extensive visas and vaccinations.

She says she didn't know, "I didn't know about the situation in Burma," but what she really means is she doesn't even know where Burma is. What countries does it touch? Do they grow rice, bananas, or both?

He says, "I remember." He remembers when all that controversy erupted, that woman, their leader, stuck in jail. But really, he doesn't know where Burma is either.

"Why didn't they just kill her?" she asks, amazed that one woman's frail body could survive the hate of an entire army. "She won the Nobel Peace Prize," he tells her. Public opinion must be taken into account. Still, she wonders how something so elusive could quiet the guns of young men eager to become heroes.

She's glad they made this movie, "so the world can learn the truth."

The world doesn't want to know the truth, he says, and she wonders why he's acting like some sort of an expert on this. "I

51

ber when all those terrorist attacks happened in Italy. . . "
she thinks, Italy? She thought his childhood was filled with
m polenta and silent churches—not terrorism.

The *Brigate Rosse*. His sister was brought in for questioning.
Coming home from school one day for lunch, he asked his mother,
"Where's Patrizia?" He wanted his big sister to help him with his
German lessons. Patrizia had been to Munich the summer before
last. "Your sister's a criminal," his mother said as she stirred the big
vat of pasta. He thought he could see tears welling up in her eyes,
but it might just have been the steam. It all turned to nothing, but
he would never forget those mid-afternoon accusations.

"Nobody really knew what was going on over there," he says,
and she thinks they probably still don't.

Aldo Moro, found dead—was it in Piazza Navona? she wonders. "No," he says. "They found him in a car, a Renault Four." It
was a well-known type of car, a car of the proletariat. The killers
parked it in the center of Rome, on a small side street half way
between the Communist party and the Christian Democrat head-
quarters. "It was symbolic," he says, but he's not quite sure of what.
"And the politicians, they knew all along where they were hiding
him. But they kept quiet." And although he says this with a laugh,
his anger is building, for this is what he hates most about his country, the keeping quiet.

She doesn't like the image of Moro slumped dead in a car,
tucked away within the mazelike streets of ancient Rome. She
prefers him in Piazza Navona, the fantastic Fountain of the Four
Rivers in the background. His body covered with a crisp white
cloth, like the ones which cover the little marble tables of the
nearby cafés, yet this one is splattered with blood.

"Why did they do it?" she asks, knowing he likes to talk about
his country, now that he's far away. "Because Moro was making
deals," he says mysteriously and thinks, if she wants more, she'll
ask. She does and he tells of Moro's efforts to forge a peace between
the Right and the Left, a peace neither side wanted. "They'd stop
him any way they could. They'd kill him if they had to."

She's a little envious of his history. Wishes she too had terrorism and red berets and siblings dangerously connected to killers and revolutionaries. It's the struggle that keeps people alive, she thinks, fighting for their lives. Once their guard is let down, once the semblance of peace and freedom exists and they have settled into an easy domesticity, they are pounced upon by an enemy who they thought had given up.

Her history of death and persecution is far away, so distant that the mention of great, great aunts and uncles escaping from Cossacks seems more of a punch line to a tasteless joke than a tragic past.

Her old and dead aunts were young then, little girls with long hair and bows. Word would come of armed men on horses, prompting families to shove all their valuables into old potato sacks and leave their homes and towns as if they were nothing but temporary encampments. As mothers packed food for the long journey they'd wonder whether their daughters would be swept up by galloping men, lost amidst the brazenness of this alien land they were forced to call home.

But it wasn't their home and maybe that's why she still can't say that her ancestors were Russian with any sort of conviction. They weren't Russian, her father used to tell her, they were Jews. "Then am I American?" she wonders. Maybe she's just biding her time in a place where at any moment she could be forced into gathering up her possessions and fleeing for her life.

He's not American, he's Italian, but he now talks about his fellow countrymen in a way only an expatriate could. He says "they" and "them" as if he were never a part of it and glad to be rid of it—and he is. He'll never go back there to live, will return as nothing more than a visitor, to see his family and bring back grappa for his in-laws. He's always envied the tourists in his country, how they come and enjoy the views, drink the wine, and stuff themselves on pasta, without ever even knowing the name of the country's prime minister, or which mobsters helped get him into office.

He won't ever become a citizen of the United States though. He wants to remain outside, a non-citizen, countryless. He'll be a visitor in his homeland, an alien in his home.

They walk and walk, forgetting about subways and buses and cabs, passing restaurants of Turkey and Vietnam and France, their hunger rising to their heads and turning into a wish for travel. They don't stop to look at any of the intriguing menus, too overwhelmed to choose only one country, only one flavor to satisfy their craving.

They're almost home when they smell the roasted pork and saffron rice of their Spanish-speaking neighbors, who serve their spicy concoctions under signs which read Mexican, Spanish, Spanish-Chinese, Tex-Mex. And behind all these permutations are histories of occupations and immigrations that they will never fully understand, that they will distinguish only by the color of the rice, the consistency of the sauce.

Only an hour has passed since they gazed through the thick green leaves of the Burmese forests and it's already becoming a dim memory. She meant to look up Burma in her atlas, place it among countries whose geography isn't so obscure, but when she gets home her mind is full of pasta and grilled cheese.

If she *had* opened her atlas, if she had found the country which sits prominently between India and Thailand, China and Bangladesh, she would have discovered that at some point between the events depicted in the movie and today, the country of Burma changed its name. Now it is called Myanmar, and the capital city of Rangoon is called Yangon. And if she would have seen it, she would have felt a great chasm open it up before her, and there she would be, teetering on the edge, for what could she have to hold onto, if not even a name did she know?

But by now the long walk home has erased all questions of far-off lands, and instead she stands in the kitchen, leaning firmly against the countertop.

"What do you want for dinner?" she asks and he replies by opening the refrigerator and staring, searching, hoping that somehow, while they've been away, something has been magically inserted into their lives—a taste, a sensation, a dream, something of which tonight, they might be able to partake.

NOT BY CHOICE

I'M FORTY-SIX YEARS OLD AND NEVER BEEN MARRIED. Not by
choice. So there you have it. Now you know it all. You can stop
right here if you want, because if what you're after is the essential
truth about Betty Watermane, you've got it already: forty-six,
never been married, not by choice.

You think I like it this way? You think I want to be defined by
such miserable little facts? Taken one by one they're all harmless
enough. Forty-six. O.K., my life's not over quite yet. Never been
married. A good percentage of the world's population falls under
that heading. Not by choice. A mere appendage, a qualifier, and
yet, full of significance in its own right. It seems my whole life is
one big fat Not By Choice. How I want to choose! But most of
all, I want to be chosen. Oh, to be chosen! I crave it beyond anything else.

The pattern started innocently enough. Last to be chosen for
the third grade kickball team, which was really not to be chosen
at all. There was the last to be chosen, then there was me. The
next big blow was the junior prom. Not a bite. Then came the
senior prom. Same story. What was wrong with me? I wondered. I
wasn't so bad looking. Had a good sense of humor. What more
could they want? Frankly, everyone was baffled, except for the

boys of course.

Then the years just kept flying by, without so much as a nibble. Sure, there were the miscellaneous dates now and then, dinners at the marina, movies at the mall, but nothing came of it.

And now here I am. Forty-six years old, never been married and most definitely, not by choice. How did it happen? Ever since I was a little girl, all I ever dreamed of was getting married and having a family. It was all any girl dreamt about. Each year it didn't happen, I just kept thinking, next year, next year. At forty I gave up on the children part. Now I'm thinking I better give up on the whole thing. It's just not going to happen. I'll die a lonely old woman. O.K., let's just lay the cards on the table. I'll die a virgin.

Do I really have to explain how such a thing could have happened? I'm not even sure that I know. What I do know is that if you make it through high school and college without so much as an open-mouthed kiss, you're pretty much cursed for the rest of your life. That's what I was, cursed. And don't you think that every man I met from age twenty-two on sensed it down to the marrow of his bones?

If only I could mourn for my missed opportunities! But, alas, I cannot. For there were none. Not a one! Could I count Henry Goldfarb's hand down my blouse in the middle of *The Godfather* as a missed opportunity? Or Steven Rinaldi pressing his erect penis against my leg at a Muscular Dystrophy dance-a-thon? These were not missed opportunities, they were simply lapses in judgment. The desperate efforts of a woman forlorn.

I considered just breaking the cycle, dropping a bit of water into the vast dustbowl which is my life, but I couldn't bring myself to actually do it. I thought about escort services, personal ads, or just going home with the next construction worker who whistled at me on the street, but after waiting this long, I somehow wanted the first time to be something special.

So I decide to confide in my friend Suzy. Needless to say I haven't been real keen on letting anybody know about this predicament of mine, but I've known Suzy for a while now and I figure she could maybe help me out, steer me in the right direction.

"Oh, Betty, I'm so sorry," says Suzy. This is good. She realizes it isn't really my fault, more like some natural disaster, an act of God.

"Yeah, well, it's time to stop crying about it and just do something."

"You're absolutely right, Betty. You've got such a great attitude."

"So what can I do?"

"Well, as I see it, you've got two problems," says Suzy. I can't believe this woman! She's already got lists drawn up in her head, plans of action, modes of recourse. Now I realize I should have come to her a long time ago.

"Two problems. Right," I say.

"First, there's the problem of wanting to be married. Now that's a problem a lot of us have, including me."

"But you were married, Suzy."

"That's true. But it was no happily-ever-after, now, was it?"

"No."

"So what I'm saying is, your first problem is something a lot of women our age are going through."

"Yeah, I guess you're right."

"Now the second problem is a little more tricky."

"You mean, the virgin part."

"Yeah," says Suzy, biting her lip and thinking hard. "The way I see it is, you've got to just go out and get that taken care of."

"You mean, like, a prostitute?"

"Oh, no! I mean, you want to just get that first time over with already. Get all that pressure out of the way."

"All right," I say, eagerly waiting to hear the rest of the plan.

"And you know, I think I've got just the guy to do it."

"Who is he?"

"His name is Marvin Kline."

Once I hear those two words, Marvin Kline, it's as if my whole life has changed. I have found the secret, the Holy Grail, the meaning of it all. Marvin Kline. He would be my deliverer, my savior from darkness, the giver of light. Finally, I know his name. I know it all. I even know when. Saturday night, the eighteenth day of the third month, nineteen hundred and ninety-five.

Getting ready for my date, I can already feel a profound difference, something I'd never felt before. It's a kind of anticipation, a
certainty that something really is going to happen. I'm dressing for
a purpose, not just going through the motions like I used to do.
And now, I finally understand. I understand the elaborate produc-
tions women go through as they ready themselves for a date. I
understand the hot oil treatments and the facial masks, leaving
skin and hair dewy and moist, soft to the touch. The careful dab-
bing of perfume all over the body, in places where the scent could
only be appreciated in the most intimate of circumstances. And
the beautiful lingerie which I had tried so hard to enjoy, convinc-
ing myself that women wore it for themselves, to feel the silkiness
against their skin, to admire themselves in their bathroom mirrors
before covering it all with heavy wools and cottons. Yes, now I
understand! I rip off the tags of my black satin underwear and bra
and put it on carefully, arranging and adjusting and yes, even
admiring. I'm looking at myself in a whole new way, because I
know that later, I will be looked at by somebody else.

He's coming to pick me up at seven and it's only six, so I pour
myself a drink. I pour a tall vodka tonic and I even have limes. I
take a sip and, oh my God, it's the best thing I've ever tasted! I
haven't eaten a whole day and I can feel the vodka going to my
head, closer and closer after every sip. It's like no drink I've ever
had in my life. How many times have I drunk this very same
drink? I've drunk it in anger and I've drunk it in boredom and I've
drunk it in gnawing, sad loneliness. But now, now it's so different.
The cool rush to my head, my cheeks warm and rising, and a
pleasant calm all around my chest and shoulders. I could stay like
this for hours. But the point is, I won't have to. Any minute he'll
be here. He'll catch me in my bliss and make it soar to new
heights.

The doorbell rings and my heart leaps. I'm nervous. The
effects of the vodka have vanished and my heart is beating rapidly,
the glass about to fall out of my sweaty palms. I didn't expect this
to happen. I wonder if perhaps I should just pretend not to be
here, forget the whole thing. Instead, I walk to the door and open

it before I can think another thought.

There he is, Marvin Kline, the man who is about to change my life forever. The first thing I see are the flowers in his hands. Orchids. Their soft purple manages to color everything else I see—the bald head, the stout figure, the narrow blue eyes, all made exotic and lovely. He's smiling, his white teeth sparkling against a complexion ruddy from work.

"Hello," he says, "I'm Marvin. Suzy's friend." His voice is low and gruff, but enormously friendly.

"Hi, I'm Betty," I say and the sound of my voice startles me. It sounds high pitched and annoying. Nasal. He must have already figured I'm not from around here.

"Nice to meet you," he says.

We're still standing in the doorway and I don't know what to do. I know I should just invite him in, but I'm suddenly stricken. I can't do it. Maybe he'll just walk on in and pour himself a drink. Yes, maybe he'll do just that.

But he doesn't. He just stands there looking at me. Staring. He's about to say something.

"You look beautiful this evening, Betty."

Good Lord! Could it be so? Could this man be for real and could he really have just told me I look beautiful this evening? I want to hug him. To shower him with kisses. To take his orchids and his compliment and wash it all down with another vodka tonic. But I just stand there. And so does he. But you see, that gives me a chance to really look at Marvin Kline. I watch him and I think, wait a minute. This is a little too good to be true. How did he know to bring orchids, my favorite flower? And how did he know to tell me I looked beautiful? My God, Suzy must have told him! Told him the whole thing. He knows what I am, and he knows what he's here for. What a fool I am!

"She told you!" I scream, and I can't believe such a sound could come out of my mouth in the presence of anyone, let alone a strange man.

"Excuse me?" he says, acting confused.

"She told you I'm a virgin!" I say and burst into tears. I cover my face in shame and run away, into my bedroom, leaving Marvin standing there in the doorway.

The bedroom is dark and stuffy, the windows closed and the shades pulled. My face is smashed up against a tear-soaked bedspread, and I can feel my clothes wrinkling, my make-up smearing. The cool breeziness of the evening seems miles away to me now, the image of Marvin Kline's sparkling smile against the star-filled sky.

I've stopped crying but I feel like crying some more. I let out a muffled moan and wait for more tears to come, but they don't, so I just lie there, left-over tears drying cold on my face.

"Betty?" I hear, coming from the hallway. Oh God, I think, and the tears begin to flow.

"Betty, are you O.K.?" He's coming towards the bedroom and I guess I'm too shocked to run into the bathroom and hide. Who cares anymore, anyway? Let him see it all. Me at my worst which is where I always seem to be.

"Can I come in?" he says, but I don't answer. So he comes over to me and sits on the edge of the bed. I'm still sobbing into the bedspread and suddenly I feel a warm hand on my back.

"Don't cry, Betty," he says, so I keep on crying. "Suzy didn't tell me anything. Really."

"Well, now you know," I say and as I do, I expose my blotchy, bloated face to poor Marvin.

Marvin takes my face in his hands and looks me right in the eyes, but doesn't say a word. Instead he gets up and goes to the bathroom, and returns with a wad of Kleenex in his hand. He holds my face again and begins wiping it off, gentle but firm, as if I were a child messy from an ice cream cone.

I look at him as he wipes, searching for evidence, evidence of his disgust, his disbelief. But I see nothing but the determination to get my face dry and clean.

"Now you know," I say, trying to provoke him, to pull out what I know is lurking behind that calm exterior.

"What do I know, Betty? That you're a virgin?"

I gulp as if the words were enough to issue forth a whole new bout of tears, but he catches me just in time.

"So what?" he says. He wipes a newly formed tear from the corner of my eye. "So what."

Before I know it, Marvin Kline's got me sitting up against the headboard of my bed, and he's sitting there right beside me. My hand is curled up inside of his and we're staring straight ahead at my dresser, the room now lit by the small reading lamp on the nightstand.

"You want me to get you a drink?" he asks me.

"Yes," I say. "A vodka tonic, please."

I sit and wait for him, listening to the ice cubes and the tonic, not thinking at all about what to do next.

He comes back with two glasses in his hands. He hands me one then sits back on the bed.

"There you go," he says. "Now drink that down."

I take a sip and continue staring straight ahead. I've never felt so comfortable in silence before.

"You feel better now?"

"Yeah. I do. Thanks."

"Good."

"Sorry to put you through all this," I say. "You should feel free to go whenever you want."

"Don't worry about me. I'm doing just fine."

"You don't think I'm some sort of freak?" I say to Marvin Kline.

"Now why would I think that?"

"Well, how many forty-six year old virgins do you know?"

"None," he says. "But that doesn't mean they're not out there."

"I don't think so," I say.

"Besides, what do you want to be like everyone else for?"

"It's not that, it's just . . . "

"What is it?"

"It just makes me feel, like I'm not good enough. You know."

"Have you ever thought that maybe you just never found anyone who's good enough for you?"

"Yeah!" I laugh. "But I figured that was an easy excuse."

"Listen, Betty. How many women do you think sleep with men they don't even like? Plenty. Brutish, inconsiderate, selfish men. And you think these women are having a good time? No! They're miserable about it. But they think it's all they deserve. All they can get. You, on the other hand, Betty, you've got standards. And for forty-six years you haven't let those standards drop for even a second."

"Well, maybe a second or two."

Marvin smiles at me and puts down his drink. He's clutching my free hand in his. "It's tough holding out like you have, Betty. Tough sticking to your principles. Don't feel ashamed. Be proud of yourself."

He takes my drink and sets it down on the nightstand next to his. He takes my other hand and holds them both together, inside his own. Then he leans forward and kisses me on the cheek. Then he kisses me on the mouth. We let go of each others hands and we put them around each others waists. Then we start kissing some more, open-mouthed, vodka tonic, tear-flavored kisses.

There I am kissing away, touching and groping and kissing, and I can't believe how easy this is. Here we are in a bed, something which seems to be made especially for this sort of activity, and it all seems so natural.

And let's just say that Marvin knows exactly what he's doing. He gets my shirt off but leaves my bra on for a while, admiring it and the way it supports my breasts, feeling the soft satin as if it were my own skin. Once my clothes are all off, he spreads me out in a most flattering position, my stomach flat against the mattress, my curled hair tumbling over the pillow. Marvin's undressed too, but he lets me get used to him before jumping on top. He's got nice broad shoulders, freckled from the sun, and a lot of black hair on his chest.

Of course, there's the main attraction, the penis, which is a nice medium—at least I think it is—because it doesn't strike me as being either under or over the norm. I imagined I'd be a little put off by the bare, commanding presence of the famous male

organ, but actually, it's kind of nice. And once we really get started, it's more than nice.

There's Marvin, working away, and I can't believe what I'm
feeling. I'm trying not to think too much about all those articles
I've read in *Cosmo* and *Mademoiselle*, but it's actually a good thing
I did read them or I might not realize that I'm about to have an
orgasm. All the laments and worries of thousands of unsatisfied
women come pouring into my head as I lie there, experiencing
what I imagine only a few blessed souls get to feel their first time
around. Marvin can tell he's doing a good job and so is going at it
with all the more vigor. He's actually smiling, watching me, and
I'm happy to be watched.

Afterwards, he lies down on top of me, still inside, and we
both continue to breathe heavily. I'm having a hard time breathing with Marvin's bulk on my chest, so he rolls over and lies
beside me.

Once I recover I turn onto my side and look at Marvin. His
breathing has returned to normal and now his eyes are closed. I
think he's sleeping.

I watch him as he sleeps and suddenly I feel like I have met
this man before. Who is this Marvin Kline? I wonder. Who is this
man who seemed so familiar to me, the moment I saw him standing outside my front door? I let him into my house, into my bedroom, into my bed, with barely an introduction, with no more
than a few words exchanged between us. How could I do such a
thing? Then I realize I could do it because I do know this man,
this Marvin Kline. He's no stranger.

I've met a million Marvin Kline's throughout my forty-six
years. In high-school, college, at the office, in bars. I've been on
dates with them, sat through movies with them, and danced with
them at Muscular Dystrophy dance-a-thons.

I turn onto my back and look up at the ceiling of my little
one bedroom apartment. It's a plain, cream-colored ceiling, low
with a white glass light fixture in the center. I had always wanted
to live in a big old house, with walls of wood and carefully carved
moldings. I dreamed of rustic wood tables and old rocking chairs

covered with quilts. I have seen houses like these, in Vermont, Northern California, and even the suburbs of Chicago. I've always known where they were, I was just waiting. Waiting for what, I don't know.

TIGHTROPE

JUNE RANDOLPH HAD LIVED ALL OF HER twenty-three years in New York City, so when she informed her parents that she and her boyfriend Robert had decided to move to Los Angeles, the news came as quite a shock. "You break out in a rash after an hour in the sun," said Mrs. Randolph, "and Robert doesn't even know how to drive!" June responded that sunscreen and driving lessons would easily accommodate for these deficiencies, and after a while, Mrs. Randolph calmed down. "Well, at least you'll have your Aunt Margaret there."

June started the packing process early, sure that it would take at least a couple of weeks to gather and arrange all of her personal effects, but soon it became clear that there really wasn't much to pack. After graduating from college a year ago, June had moved right back into her parents apartment on the Upper West Side, and so hadn't had the opportunity to buy her first full size bed, or shop the cramped West Village antique stores for night tables and throw pillows. It was just as well, thought June, for what she and Robert wanted was a fresh start.

Both June and Robert had gone to high school at Dalton, but hadn't really gotten to know each other until their senior year at Columbia. In the weeks before graduation the two talked incessantly of travel through Africa and South America, or at least a ride down the Oregon coast. But when both received low paying jobs at high caliber companies immediately after graduation, they couldn't really refuse. "You'll take a trip next summer," counseled Mrs. Randolph. "Now it's time to get started on your careers."

After only a year working as a photographer's assistant at *Vanity Fair,* June was already burnt out. Of course there was the initial thrill of meeting movie stars and models, literary greats, and billionaires, but soon those glamorous icons became nothing but needy and cumbersome mounds of flesh which June was responsible for feeding with pasta salad, watering with Evian, and transporting to studios and location sites. June had often thought that she might like being an art director on films, and so one day decided that Los Angeles was really the place to be. It didn't take much to convince Robert to leave his job in investment banking and come along with her. He thought he might even like to work with June, in the movies.

"Are you sure you want to do this, Robert?" asked Mrs. Randolph.

"I'm really not happy with my job."

They were all sitting in the Randolphs' courtyard on yellow cushioned wicker chairs, lemonades and vodka tonics sitting with a surprising steadiness on the rippled surface of the table. June was looking up at the tall brick building which blocked the late afternoon sun.

"Well, I hope you're not just giving everything up for June."

"Of course not," said Robert. "I want to go."

June noticed a little blond-haired girl standing on one of the terraces which overlooked the private courtyard, but she couldn't seem to recognize the girl. Where did she come from? wondered June. Who was her mother? She thought she knew everyone who lived in the tightly knit buildings which surrounded her home.

"Are you sure you can't find some of that film work here in New York?" Mr. Randolph turned to June. "I just read in the *Times* today about some movie they're shooting in Battery Park."

"That's not the point, Daddy," said June, not taking her eyes off the little girl above. "Robert and I want to get away, try something new."

"Well, your Aunt Margaret has already told me that she's thrilled to put you both up for as long as you need," said Mrs. Randolph.

June watched as the little girl hung from the black iron rail which encompassed the terrace. She was looking down at the Randolphs. Then a plane flew by and the girl abruptly looked up, trying to place the loud roar of the jet. She let go of the bar with one hand, and pointed at the passing airplane, her balance thrown. June wondered at what point she should leap out of her chair and stand beneath the girl, poised to break her fall.

"Thank goodness for Margaret," said Mrs. Randolph. "Please, June, promise me you'll call her right when you get there."

The little girl's mother rushed out of the apartment and onto the terrace, grabbing the little girl and giving her a light slap on her rear. June recognized the woman and remembered that, yes, she did have a daughter.

"Don't worry, Mrs. Randolph," said Robert. "We'll be fine."

"Oh, I know. It's so exciting. California!"

June had become increasingly quiet during the days which led up to her departure, and when the big day finally came, she was downright solemn. She didn't help Robert load up the car at all, and when her mother asked if she could make them some sandwiches for the trip, she simply turned away and left the room. Mrs. Randolph wasn't concerned though, for she knew her daughter to be moody at times.

June was in her bedroom, packing up some last minute things, when her mother walked in carrying her portfolio.

"You almost forgot this." Mrs. Randolph held the large black leather case out to her daughter.

"Yeah, well, I wasn't planning on bringing it. There's nothing any good in there anyway."

"What do you mean? You have to bring it if you hope to find

any sort of real job out there."

Mrs. Randolph tucked the portfolio under June's arm. The leather was cold against her skin. She looked at her mother for something more.

"You should get going, June. I don't want you out on the highway late at night."

By the time Robert finished saying his good-byes to the Randolphs and turned towards the car, June was already behind the wheel, arms stretched forward, eyes staring straight ahead. June's stare was not fixed on anything in particular, only squinting into the bright sun, for she knew that her destination was too far in the distance to even begin to imagine.

June navigated through the crowded streets of New York with an expertise that Robert could not help admiring. It was a pride only someone who had never sat behind the wheel himself could feel. For a New Yorker not to know how to drive was not so unusual, but Robert could not help noticing the questioning glances and suspicious smiles which often greeted such a trivial piece of information. He knew someday he'd learn, but wasn't in any big hurry.

As they drove west through New Jersey, the signs along the highway were like landmarks to the couple's own histories. Robert's grandmother lived in Newark, and Paterson was where Mr. Randolph grew up. And the little town right on the border between New Jersey and Pennsylvania was where the Randolphs spent their summers and Robert became part of the family.

After three hours of driving, they finally stopped at a McDonald's for a bite to eat.

"How you doing?" asked Robert. He put his hand to June's cheek.

"O.K.," said June who quickly raised her chicken sandwich to her mouth. Robert turned back to his own lunch.

"I'm sorry I can't help you out with the driving."

"It's fine."

"You're not having any second thoughts about this, are you?" asked Robert.

"No," said June. "Why?"

"I don't know. You seem not so into it anymore."

"No, I'm fine, really. I'm glad we're getting out of New York."

"Yeah, me, too."

While they had never actually been to the west coast, had never been further west then Ohio for that matter, June and Robert were sure they'd fit right in. Los Angeles was busy and cosmopolitan, just like New York, but with better weather and more space. Yet between these two outposts of diverse culture and professional opportunity lay an entire country yet to be traversed.

June had always wanted to travel across America, to drive through the rolling green hills of Pennsylvania, the cornfields of Kansas, the Arizona desert. But actually being there in the car, speeding away from her home, her past, into the nebulous blur of her future in California, she found herself unable to enjoy the journey.

Robert would gaze out of his window, mesmerized by the stunning scenery, lulled into a peaceful reverie by the gentle hum of the car's engine, while June sat stiff in the driver's seat, her face flushed from the heat of the sun. After hours of staring mindlessly forward, she would find her hands clutching the steering wheel, the sweat dripping from the light blue vinyl.

When evening finally came, June was filled with relief, eager to close her eyes, to release her body from the vise which seemed to have been gripping it a whole day long.

They went to the hotel restaurant for dinner, where Robert ordered the half roast chicken and June had a bowl of vegetable soup. When they got back to their room, June lay down on the bed while Robert went into the bathroom to clean up. June was tired, but she still hoped that Robert would come out of the bathroom soon and that he would want to make love to her. She longed for the feeling of letting go, of having someone else control her movements and feelings. Robert came out and sat next to her on the bed. He began removing her clothes and kissing her, and as his hands glided over her body, June could feel her muscles relaxing and rising of their own free will.

As the two traveled further into the Midwest, June and Robert's status as New Yorkers became more and more of an issue. Without having to open their mouths, the bright orange license plates on the front and back of their car screamed out New York to all who cared to listen. And in almost every diner, gas station, and motel there always seemed to be someone at least mildly interested in the place of origin of these two youngsters.

"Where you all comin' from," asked the waitress at the Blue Diner.

"New York City," responded Robert with as much enthusiasm as he could muster.

"Uh, huh," the waitress said with interest. "Never had much desire to go to New York, I must say."

June looked at Robert and shrugged.

"Yeah," said the waitress, confirming her own suspicions, "I think that place is just a little too much for the likes of me."

"Too much, that's what it is," said Robert cheerily.

"Guess that means Kansas is just too little!" and the waitress let out a shriek of laughter.

June did her best to smile.

"Aawww," the waitress was still smiling to herself. "Too little," and she shook her head. She straightened herself up. "What can I get you folks?"

"What's the special today?" asked Robert.

"Biscuits and gravy," said the waitress.

"O.K., what the hell, biscuits and gravy it is."

"What color gravy you want?" The waitress was staring down at her pad.

"What colors you got?" asked Robert.

"White and brown."

"Oh. I think I'll have to go with brown."

"And you, miss?"

"I'll have scrambled eggs," said June.

The waitress stood staring at her pad, seemingly waiting for something more.

"Do those come in different colors, too?" asked June.

"No, just one," said the waitress. "What kind of toast you want?"

"Wheat, please, and coffee."

"Me, too," said Robert.

The waitress left.

Robert sat and looked at June who was staring down at the table. The waitress came back and poured their coffee.

After another minute in silence, Robert spoke.

"What's the matter, June?"

The moment the words were out, June heaved in a mouthful of air which seemed to then push forward the tears which had been waiting patiently at the surface. June sat silently, a steady stream of tears running down her face.

"Did I do something?" asked Robert.

June shook her head.

The waitress came back and brought their food. She looked at June for a moment then quickly turned away.

"Please, June, tell me."

June dried her cheeks with a paper napkin and blew her nose. "I'm sorry, Robert, I don't know what's the matter with me. I think maybe I just don't feel so great."

"Then maybe we should stop for a while."

"Oh, no. I'll be fine. Really. Don't worry."

Once they were back on the road, a strange feeling came over June. She guessed the feeling had really started from the moment they left the city, only she had been trying her best to push it back. She did have responsibilities. But somehow, driving through the barren plains of Kansas, the impossibly level road stretching out and disappearing into an all too near horizon, June felt as if she would at any moment drive off the end of the earth.

She drove along the endless road, the road which did not vary, looking for clues. She waited impatiently for the bright green signs which would give her information, what towns they were passing, how many miles to the next exit, what kinds of restaurants or gas stations they might hope to find there. But it wasn't enough. She needed more.

As she sped forth, June could not help feeling the car hurtling towards some terrible abyss, and here she was, guiding it, accelerating herself and another into the very place they should have been avoiding.

She looked over at Robert for a sign, some kind of signal which would tell her what to do. But Robert was serenely staring out his window, completely unaware of his terrible fate.

June began gasping for air as if she were drowning. She tried to grab the steering wheel but her arms went limp, her hands, drenched with sweat, could no longer grip. She could feel the speed inside her, her own body accelerating forward, uncontrollably, as if she were falling. Suddenly, she saw an exit and before she knew what was happening, swerved to the right and fled the highway. Once on the exit road, June felt relief, as if she had escaped the worst possible doom. But when Robert turned to her with his frightened, questioning eyes, June knew she had escaped nothing.

"What happened?"

"I don't know," said June quietly. She stopped the car at the end of the road and they both sat in silence.

Suddenly, June burst out into tears, not the silent ones of that morning, but loud hysterical sobs. She gasped for air only to transform it into a terrible moan which emanated from deep within.

Robert moved near her and took June in his arms. He held her tightly, and the more he squeezed, the more June's pain poured forth.

"I'm sorry," June said in between sobs. "I'm so sorry."

Robert held her and waited. After a time, he felt he should say something.

"We don't have to go any further, June. We can just stay here . . . in Wichita, and build a life for ourselves."

Having regained some composure, June looked up at Robert and smiled. It was the first smile Robert had seen for days and he wanted it never to leave.

"O.K.? How about it?" he asked.

At that moment, June knew it was with him she must spend the rest of her life.

"Hi, Mom, it's me," June wondered whether her voice was too shaky.

"Hi!" said Mrs. Randolph ecstatically. She detected nothing. "Where are you?"

"Wichita."

"Yeah? And how's it going?"

"Fine."

"Great!" Mrs. Randolph waited a moment, then continued. "And how's Robert?"

"Fine." Realizing she had better say more, she added, "He's doing fine."

"Well, I'm so glad," said Mrs. Randolph. "We were getting a little worried about you guys."

"Mom," this set June off, "why do you have to worry? There's nothing to worry about. We're fine."

"It's my job to worry."

"Well please just stop it. I don't need that. I just don't need to hear that." June felt her throat tighten. "I better get going."

"Have you eaten yet?"

"No. No, we have to go eat now."

"All right. Will you call tomorrow?"

"I don't know. Just don't worry if I don't."

"O.K., I won't."

"Bye, Mom."

"O.K. Be careful."

The journey through Oklahoma, Texas, Arizona, was like a dream, full of stops and starts and swerves off of the sinister high- ways onto the relatively safe roads of the towns and cities which

73

dotted the interstate. June couldn't seem to handle the openness of the highway, the forward motion without end, her tires almost floating above the road, speeding towards nothing. It was like skidding along a great big tightrope, where the slightest misstep would hurl her into oblivion. So June gravitated towards the urban centers, with their stop signs and traffic lights to guide her, restrict her, pull her down to the ground. And at each town that rescued June from her terror, Robert offered the same thing.

"If you want, we can settle right here. Make a life for ourselves," Robert took June's damp chin in his hand. "Right here in Tucamcari, New Mexico, we'll start a brand new life."

June and Robert went into the nearest diner, took a local newspaper off of the rack and sat down in a booth. They opened it up to the real estate section and were pleased to find extremely reasonable rents there in Tucamcari. They laughed over the mansion they were sure to find for a mere three hundred dollars a month. Tomorrow morning they'd go look for jobs.

When the waitress came over they both ordered the daily special, chicken parmigiana with pasta, soup, and salad for $5.95.

"Where you all from?" asked the waitress.

"We live here," smiled June.

It took June only three days to find a job with a landscaping company. People in that part of New Mexico preferred the lush creations of professional landscapers to the dry, sparse plant life which grew naturally around their homes. A week later Robert landed a position as a computer consultant. While Robert didn't necessarily know that much about computers, it seemed he knew more than most people in Tucamcari. Both were making decent salaries and were quite content with their chosen professions.

But June couldn't quite bring herself to tell her parents of her and Robert's change of plans. So she lied and told them they were staying temporarily at a cheap hotel in Hollywood.

"Why on earth are you doing that?" demanded Mrs. Randolph. "Why don't you call Margaret? I told you she's happy to put you up."

June told her mother that there was a line waiting to use the phone. She really had to go.

"Well, is there some way I can reach you?"

"No," insisted June, saying goodbye and hanging up before Mrs. Randolph could question any more.

Whenever June spoke to her mother during those first weeks in New Mexico, she felt that familiar vice take hold of her. While Mrs. Randolph urged her to phone her aunt Margaret, to relinquish herself to the authority of her mother's sister, June felt herself back on that tightrope, the one which stretched across the country, from her home in New York City, to Aunt Margaret's house in Los Angeles. And as she carefully tip-toed along, she experienced the intense dizziness of her inevitable fall.

But June had chosen to jump before falling, and had landed safe and sound in Tucamcari, New Mexico.

"You should tell your mother," Robert said, "The longer you wait, the worse it'll be."

June knew he was right. So she called her mother and told her the truth.

"How could you?" asked Mrs. Randolph, and June wondered if her mother was referring to the lie she had told or the fact that she was "throwing her life away" in the desert of New Mexico. But when June finally hung up after an hour of listening to her mother cry and scold, she realized that it really didn't matter.

A VIOLENT LIFE

I COME TO THE DINING HALL WHERE THE MONKS used to eat every day now. Not for nourishment, for the kitchens have long closed, but to gaze at a depiction of the most famous meal in all of history. It is a tiny room, and I wonder how many monks could have been squeezed into it, and where they found the space to keep the stoves to bake their bread, the pots to boil their porridge. Yet they call this mere slip of a room a museum, a museum devoted to Andrea del Castagno.

The front door to the museum is nothing grand, smaller even than the doors which lead into most Florentine apartments, and it has a tiny metal plaque outside which is easy to miss if you're not looking. If you dare to open this unwelcoming door, you'll find a lone old man on guard. He's sitting on a rickety wooden school chair and waiting patiently for his lunch break which is scheduled to last four hours. He's already planning to come back late if his wife has prepared tiramisu as she's promised. He'll have to take a little nap after that. It doesn't really matter if he's late because no one ever comes here, anyway.

Except me, because like I said, I come here every day. I can tell the guard is annoyed, wishes he had his little museum to himself once again, hopes this silly little American girl will quickly finish up her Italian lessons and go back home. But I'm no college student, I'm a grown woman, already married and divorced. And I can stay in Italy as long as I like, because there's nothing to go back to anymore.

When I told my friend Ginnie I was moving to Italy, she said, "You're going to let him chase you out of the country?" I knew that's what people thought, but I didn't come here to get away from my ex-husband. I'm not afraid of him. I don't care if I run into him at the grocery store, arm in arm with the woman he left me for. What my husband did was all too typical. Betrayed wives like me are a dime a dozen. Of course that didn't make me feel any less like I was being suffocated, slowly—a fluffy down pillow being smashed against my face by the familiar man sleeping in my bed.

During my first two weeks in Florence I carried around my Michelin guide like it was a bible. I circled the city like a lioness scouting out her prey, preparing to consume the great works of the Renaissance. It was all so beautiful—the statues, the church-es, the grand piazzas—but for some reason all that beauty left me cold. The smooth porcelain cheeks of the David, the silence of the great, cavernous Duomo. That calm, placid serenity seemed to taunt me, and it was all I could do to keep myself from sitting down in a pew and screaming.

After two weeks I left my Michelin guide in a café and began wandering the streets aimlessly. The problem was that I could never seem to get lost in this perfect little metropolis, and I always found myself back at a familiar landmark. Until the day I discovered my museum.

The guard nods at me when I arrive in the morning, a cour-tesy even he cannot begrudge someone as diligent as I. I step into the main room and hide my eyes until I'm smack in the middle, then turn toward the wall and let the vision of the main fresco hit me with full force. The first thing I notice is the color—the magnificent reds, rich and lush and flowing like an aged burgundy across the well-preserved wall. So much red! Even the blues and the greens and the golds seem to be just a lot of shades of red. Then my eye runs along the smooth white cloth which covers the table, uncluttered, with not a morsel of food, not a wrinkle to threaten its perfect line. The apostles sit quietly in their seats, contemplating the fate of their beloved master who sits so close, yet seems to them unreachable. None of the melodramatic gestures of DaVinci's more famous execution, the intricate bundles of threes, crowding and confronting Christ like a rabid mob. No, these saintly men stay seated and quiet, yet beneath their subtle, delicate expressions lies a piercing agony which threatens to strangle their composure soon enough.

And then there is the triumph of the composition: Judas Iscariot sitting in profile, on the opposite side of the table! He sits on the side nearest me, the viewer, closer in distance to Christ than any of the others, yet blocked by the bulk of the weighty piece of furniture. How ingenious! Christ has just announced that one of his faithful apostles will betray him, and I wonder, does anyone notice who sits apart? Does anyone notice whose hideous, misshapen nose is exaggerated in profile? Does anyone notice the great chunk of marble which hangs over Judas' head, the one colored with the most fiery, damning red of all?

And so everyday I come back, and I wish this could be my home. I wish this were my dining room and I could eat in front of this fresco and maybe sleep here, too. I keep coming back because every time I leave, every time I tear my eyes away and look at something else, I feel an emptiness deep in my gut. I've come to need those brazen reds, that swirling marble, those stiff backed saints looking sad and forlorn. For now it is all I need.

Until the one day when my visit is interrupted. First I hear the guard's wooden chair scrape against the floor, as if it were screeching out, desperately trying to stop the influx of some thirty American students and an art history teacher. Before I know it they're pouring into the room, pushing me to the back, the sanctity of the museum killed by the sounds of rustling backpacks and giggles and squeaky sneakers.

They look for a moment at the different frescoes which line the walls, but once their teacher takes his position in the front of the room and opens his mouth, their eyes fall effortlessly on him.

The teacher starts rambling on and the students keep looking at him, rarely allowing their gaze to drift up to the paintings under discussion. What power the word has over the image. Just watch how people in museums carefully read the typed cards stuck to the sides of the works, then move on after barely a glance, only stopping if the name they read is sufficiently familiar.

"Now can anyone tell me what our friend Vasari has to say about Castagno?"

Vasari? Who's that? I watch curiously as all the students begin riffling through their little Penguin paperbacks looking for the answer.

Suddenly, someone shouts: "He was a murderer!"

I contain myself, waiting patiently for the teacher to correct this silly boy's mistake, but instead I hear: "Good, Robert."

What's going on here? Who is this Vasari person to accuse my artist of murder? This alleged teacher isn't even going to explain the accusation and he's already started spewing out words like perspective and foreshortening and I can tell he can't even see this painting.

I have to leave. I practically run out of the room and the guard looks at me and nods, even bigger than usual, as if to say, "Yes, I don't blame you, I wish I could leave, too." But I haven't the time for such camaraderie. I've got to find a copy of this slanderer Vasari's book.

I go to the English language bookstore, which is really just a Penguin paperback outlet, and I immediately find what I'm looking for. Two volumes—I buy both—and even after forking over 40,000 lira I leave the store feeling like a thief.

Next door is a café. I go in and get a seat, not even bothering to ask how much they'll charge me for drinking a cappuccino in one of their velvet cushioned booths. I quickly place my order then open to the table of contents. There he is, Andrea del Castagno. But what's this? He has to share his measly little ten page chapter with some guy named Domenico Veneziano? I'm already turning indignant.

*

I cannot at all think it is possible to express in words how shameful it is for a person of excellence to possess the vice of envy, and how wicked and horrible it is, under the guise of pretended friendship, to destroy not only the fame and glory of someone else, but his very life as well. For this kind of wickedness defeats all the skill and resources of language, no matter how eloquent. Therefore, without lingering over the matter, I shall simply say here and now that in people of that kind there must reside a spirit not only inhuman and fierce but utterly cruel and devil-ish, and so alien to all virtue that they cannot be thought of as animals, let alone as men, and they are not worthy to live.

My God, Andrea! What have you done? I want not to believe this, to write this man off as just a misinformed academic looking for attention. But I can't. I look at the first page and read that this Vasari was an artist who lived in Tuscany in the six-teenth century. He knows what he's talking about, this Giorgio Vasari, knew the artists or knew the people who knew the artists, their children and grandchildren and the students who carried on their work. He speaks the truth! I quickly return to Andrea's story, frightened yet eager to discover the course of his downfall.

Castagno was left fatherless and was taken by one of his uncles who kept him guarding his herds. He began to scratch drawings of animals and figures, such that everyone seeing them was filled with wonder.

Yes! This is the Andrea I know, who kept everyone filled with wonder, even as a young boy. So what happened? Could it have all started with the death of his father?

Thus the fame of this new study of Andrea's began to spread among local peasants and it came to the ears of a Florentine gentleman, called Bernardetto de' Medici who took him with him to Florence. As a result, pursuing the art of painting, and giving himself over completely to its study, Andrea showed the most perfect understanding of its problems, and especially drawing. Yet he was then not so successful in coloring his works, which he made somewhat crude and harsh, greatly diminishing their grace and excellence, and, above all, the kind of loveliness which his coloring lacks.

Accusations of envy, hypocrisy, even murder I can handle. But to say that my artist did not know the first thing about coloring is intolerable! How can I read any further? How can I trust a word this man says after so base a description of Andrea's glorious colors? But I do . . .

. . . he was commissioned to paint a part of the main chapel, of which another part had been allotted to Alesso Baldovinetti and the third part to the then very celebrated painter Domenico Veneziano, who had been brought to Florence because of the new method he had of coloring in oil. Then, while each one of them was attending to his own work, Andrea conceived a great envy for Domenico, because although he knew that he himself had more excellence in drawing, he none the less resented a foreigner such as Domenico being warmly treated and looked after by the citizens; and on account of this, the anger and contempt he felt grew so strong that he began to think how, in one way or another, he would get rid of him. And so determined to accomplish through deception and treachery what he could not do openly without obvious risk, he pretended to be very friendly towards Domenico, a good and loving person who delighted in playing the lute and sang to music and who therefore gladly accepted Andrea's friendship, in the belief that he was a very talented and amusing person. So this friendship, on the one side true, on the other feigned, continued its course, and every night the two men would come together to entertain and serenade their mistresses, much to the delight of Domenico, who being honestly fond of Andrea, taught him the method of coloring in oil, which was not yet known in Tuscany.

Of course! It had to be true. For the sake of his art, his color, Andrea would trick Domenico into revealing his secret technique. But why, why must he kill him? Why such vengeful hate from a man so talented and charmed?

*

. . . blinded by his envy of the praises that he heard of Domenico's talent, he determined to get rid of him; and having thought of many different methods of doing this, he adopted one of them as follows . . .

—Andrea, my dear man! Put down your drawing and come out with me. It's a beautiful summer's night and I'm sure we'll be able to find us a couple of *belle fanciulle* with whom we might share some wine.

—No, Domenico. I must finish before morning. Please, you go on ahead without me.

—*Merde!*

—Domenico! It's not like you to swear.

—Only when I am denied the happy company of my gentle friend am I possessed with the desire to curse.

—I'm sorry, good Domenico. Another time.

And so Domenico took his lute and left the inner chambers of Santa Maria Nuova, while Andrea remained at his desk, hunched over his sketches, working vigorously until the clock struck midnight.

Knowing that Domenico always took those twelve resounding notes as a signal to head home, Andrea hurried out of his room and into the warm night air. Having accompanied Domenico on most of his evening jaunts, Andrea knew exactly his customary way home. So he waited patiently behind the corner of a nearby building, but not before he had removed from his inner garments, a pair of leaden weights.

After a mere five minutes of waiting, but what seemed like hours to Andrea, Domenico's high pitched lute could be heard from a short distance. It was a tune Andrea knew well, something Domenico had invented himself, and as he fingered the metal weights in his moist hands, he shut his eyes tight, trying to extinguish the cheerful song from his head. But the tune just kept getting louder and louder, until it was as clear and close as Andrea's own breath, which was coming faster and more irregular as each second passed.

Finally, when he thought he could see the dust being kicked up by Domenico's boots, when he believed he could feel the spray of saliva shoot out of his lute, Andrea jumped out from behind the corner building and swung the leaden weights hard against Domenico's middle. Domenico collapsed into the street and Andrea, fearing the deed had not yet been done, beat him savagely about the head with the same leaden weights until he showed no sign of movement.

Andrea then quickly returned to his study, leaving his door ajar, and seated himself at his desk in exactly the same position as before. After a while Andrea heard a commotion in the corridors. The servants were wailing and crying and were coming toward his door.

—Master Andrea! Your beloved Domenico has been murdered!

Andrea followed the servants to the site of the brutal crime and was now able to see his gruesome handiwork by the light of the mourners' candles. He then fell to the ground, took bloody Domenico in his arms, and for the next hour cried out over and over, "Oh alas, my brother, alas, my brother!" And not a one could console him from his grief.

. . . *it was never discovered who had done him to death. And if Andrea had not revealed it in confession when he himself was nearing death, it would still not be known.*

The next day I return to my museum, the old man seemingly recovered from the American students' visit. I wish I could say the same. I go into the room and look at my fresco and of course, it's changed. As always the first thing I notice is the color, the many shades of red, but now instead of calling to mind sweet burgundies, it all appears bloody and tainted. Crude and harsh and violent were the words Vasari used to describe Andrea's work, and these words now seem carved into the painting, disfiguring it like the scratches and smears made by a gang of angry youths.

Still, for a moment I am tempted by its beauty, seduced by

the passionate note of betrayal which lies hidden beneath the surface. What kind of a life creates something as magnificent as this? A violent life? A life of intensity—volatile and uneven. A life that doesn't concern itself with societal graces, an imposed morality which clashes with its natural, dynamic course. No matter what I have learned about my beloved artist, the yearning I feel to somehow embrace his tainted image remains, and suddenly I realize that there is no reward in playing by the rules.

I'm back home now, America, and I know I said I'd never return. Of course it wasn't Andrea del Castagno which sent me back, but I'd like to believe he had something to do with it. I've done a little research about my artist, who remains always, my artist. It seems Giorgio Vasari was renowned for making things up and that art historians have been having a wonderful time for the past four hundred years trying to discount his statements.

There are those who write about Andrea del Castagno, assuming that what Vasari said was true. They enjoy playing amateur psychoanalysts, attributing his powerful colors, his dramatic brush strokes, his bold lines to the mind of a killer. And just as Vasari predicted: . . . *his dark crime overshadowed and buried his splendid talent.* But then there are those who revel in showing Vasari up. One has even proven that Andrea could not have murdered Domenico, for he died years earlier, at the tender age of twenty-six.

When I called my ex-husband he seemed glad that I was back in the country, "safe," he said. He insisted on beginning his alimony payments right away and I told him it was his choice. "I hope we can stay friends," he said, "even after all that's happened." He wants to bury my rage under a thick coat of cordiality. Who am I to refuse him?

The italicized portions of this story were taken from Giorgio Vasari's *Lives of the Artists*.

I'LL SEE YOU LATER

MR. EDWARD WATTS WALKS INTO THE BLUE PARROT SMILING. He has no qualms about smiling for no reason, like some people, because life to him is basically happy, so why not smile? He's wearing his blue and white striped seer sucker suit, the one his ex-wife Nedda hates. He always tries to dress appropriately, and what could be more appropriate for the Blue Parrot? First of all, it's blue, secondly, the Blue Parrot has sort of a tropical atmosphere. The chairs are made of wicker, and you don't want to sit in a wicker chair with a wool suit. Eddie, that's what all his friends call him, has only been to the Blue Parrot once before, but that was with his wife a long time ago, so it doesn't count. They went with their good friends the Jordans and it was not a very pleasant experience. Nedda got her panty hose caught on a stray piece of wicker right when she sat down, and she wouldn't shut up about her pair of ruined five-dollar-and-forty-nine-cent panty hose the whole night. Eddie hates panty hose. He would tell Nedda that only old ladies still wear them. And what made it even worse was she wore the kind with the girdle built in. Eddie always thought girdles were unfair. If you got fatty, bulgy thighs you shouldn't be able to hide it, you should have to live with it. He told Nedda she was living a lie.

Eddie has always been proud of his body. He goes to the gym

three times a week after work and says he doesn't know one fifty-two-year-old man with a tighter stomach. Sometimes he tells people to punch him as hard as they can to prove it. Nedda always hated when he did that, but Eddie figured she was just jealous because he weighs less than she does.

"Good evening, sir."

"Why, hello there, young lady. Beautiful night isn't it?"

"Sure is. Can . . . "

"Plenty of stars out tonight."

"Yes. Can I get you a table this evening or will you just be having a drink?"

"How about both. Can you arrange that for me?"

"I'll see what I can do," the girl says smiling wide for Eddie. Eddie can tell he's already won her over and she's thinking the same. "Will it just be one tonight?"

"Looks like it, unless you have someone in mind for me?" Eddie winks at her but not too obviously. Eddie has a nice, subtle, natural wink.

"Not yet, but I'll keep my eye out."

"Good deal."

"Come right with me and I'll show you to your table." The girl walks cautiously across the floor. She's been taught to be careful about where she seats singles. You don't want to isolate them but you don't want to put them where they'll be too conspicuous, either. "How's this?"

"Actually, I'd prefer something over there." Eddie points to an empty table right by the bar, "If it wouldn't be too much trouble."

"Not at all."

Eddie sits down in the chair facing the bar, and as he eases himself into it, careful not to snag his suit, he notices the thin brown legs jutting out from the girls red cotton dress. For a second, Eddie thinks she looks like a cherry popsicle and is about to tell her because he thinks it would make her laugh. Then he thinks better of it.

"Enjoy your meal."

"I'll try."

                 *   *   *

"How long have you folks been married?"

"Go ahead and guess, Lulu."

"Well it couldn't be more than, oh . . . fifteen years?"

"Twenty-five."

"You're kidding?"

"Nupe," Eddie shook his head, closing his eyes to Lulu's disbelief, as if his modesty forced him to repel her compliment.

Nedda and Eddie decided not to make too big a deal of their twenty-fifth anniversary and just went to their favorite chicken joint, Barney's, to celebrate. Eddie suggested it because "shelling out a hundred bucks for three bites of overcooked veal drowned in wine is no way to spend your anniversary." Nedda conceded and told him she "never much liked French food anyway." Eddie did not expect this lack of opposition so continued his argument. "And those damned waiters think I'm some sort of idiot just because I don't say that word 'pollet' right. Why can't they just call it chicken, anyway?" Nedda didn't answer. She just looked at Eddie, smiled, and went upstairs to put on a pair of slacks. She was disappointed that she couldn't wear her new green silk dress, but her birthday was coming up soon anyway.

"Ya'll have any kids?" Lulu asked, deciding to break her ready-to-take-your-order position. She didn't want to rush the Wattses.

"Two."

"Jonathon's at Yale law school and Meg is an associate producer for a news show in Dallas, Texas. We're hoping she'll take a job around here, though, so . . . "

"Nedda," Eddie gave his wife his "I don't think they really want to hear about our kids" look, which silenced Nedda immediately.

"Well, that's great!" Lulu saw the look, too.

"I guess you know what we want, Lulu. Bring us a coupla orders of chicken and some home fries."

"You got it, Mr. Watts," Lulu took their menus and headed

straight back to the kitchen, avoiding the gaze of her other customers so she could put the order in right away.

Eddie stared down at the red and white table cloth thinking
about how nice the people are at Barney's. He then looked up at
his wife. "You wanted chicken didn't you?"

"Sure," said Nedda. "Yeah."

* * *

Eddie's gotten used to going out by himself and he always says
he doesn't mind it at all. He likes watching the people. There's a
woman sitting on the other side of the bar, directly facing Eddie.
She has thick, long, dark hair and a dark complexion. With her
right hand she strokes the rim of her glass, filled with scotch and
soda, Eddie thinks, and in her left hand she holds a long
cigarette, just newly lit. She is looking down into her drink,
oblivious to the commotion around her. A young man in a blue
blazer is eyeing her, opening his mouth slightly every once in a
while as if he wants to say something, but she will not look away
from the light brown liquid. She raises her drink to her brown
lips, still looking inside the glass, and as she lowers it she slowly
brings the cigarette to her mouth and inhales deeply. Closing her
eyes, she exhales.

"Can I get you a drink?"

"Huh?"

"Can I get you a cocktail, sir?"

"Yes. A drink, yes. Uh, scotch and soda, please."

"Comin' right up."

"Thank you."

Eddie averts his gaze from the bar to the door, watching the
hostess greeting the parties eagerly. Two gentlemen walk in, one
patting the other on the back, laughing at a joke the other just
told. It is Stan Peterson, a business associate of Eddie's. Before he
can turn away, Stan catches Eddie's eye and grins, lifting his hand
up but not waving. Leaving his friend under the care of the hostess, Stan proceeds to Eddie's table, Eddie rising to greet him.

"How's it goin', Ed, old bud?" he shakes his hand firmly.

"Great, Stan. Say, did that Anderson fella call you about set-ting something up with his client? I told him you'd take care of it."

"Yeah. I'll tell you, though, I don't trust that guy as far as I can throw him."

"Know what you mean, but we can't ignore his offer."

"I hear ya. You here by yourself?"

"Yeah, just stopped in for a quick bite."

"Listen Ed, I haven't had a chance to tell you how sorry I was to hear about you and Nedda. I just couldn't . . ."

"Thanks, Stan, but really, it was a good thing."

"So you're doin' O.K.?"

"Great, I've really never felt better."

"And Nedda?"

"Good, just talked to her. Real good."

"Glad to hear it old boy. Say, why don't you join us? It's real-ly . . ."

"No, no, thanks, anyway. Just here for a quick bite. Thanks."

"O.K. You change your mind and . . ." Stan gestures to some imaginary table.

"Thanks. Gimme a call when you get it set with Anderson."

"Sure thing. I'll see you later." They shake firmly.

Eddie sits down and as he watches Stan's back he remembers the woman at the bar. She's still caressing a full glass, her long cigarette just newly lit.

*   *   *

"Hello?"

"Meg? Meg, you still there?"

"Yeah."

"Can I speak to your mother, Meg?"

"Yeah."

Eddie looked up at a spider crawling down the beige wall of his hotel room as he waited for Nedda to come to the phone. It seemed an eternity until he finally heard her short gasp for air on the other end.

"Hello." Her voice sounded hoarse and scratchy.

"What's the matter?" Eddie said, before he could think again and stop himself.

Nedda cleared her throat. "Nothing."

"Oh. I," Eddie cleared his throat, "uh called, to see how you were. Say hi or something."

"How's the hotel?" Nedda was trying to gain her composure.

"Oh great." The spider was getting dangerously close to the bed. "They got a good coffee shop. It's O.K. for now at least."

"Good."

"Yeah."

"Um, you, um, left your gym bag in the closet. I thought you'd probably want it."

"Oh, well, that's O.K., I can just get a new one."

"A new one?" Nedda's voice was beginning to tremble.

"Well, I just thought . . . "

"You're going to go buy . . . buy a new one?"

"Or I could pick it up next week if that's O.K. with you? If you don't mind."

"I don't care."

Silence. "How's Meg?"

"Fine."

"Heard from Jonathon lately? I think . . . "

"Eddie, I have to go now. I'll talk to you later. Bye."

Eddie heard the click on the other end, but it took him a few seconds to realize Nedda had hung up. The receiver still in his hand, he noticed the spider on the wall, resting. Holding it a foot away from the creature, he carefully lined the receiver up with the wall and squashed the bug. He didn't even bother wiping off the spider innards that remained. He'd let the maid take care of it later.

* * *

"I'm sorry it took me so long to get over here. I've been absolutely swamped!"

"No problem. I'm just relaxing, enjoying the view," Eddie says, turning his head back and forth. "I'm surprised it's so busy on a Wednesday night."

"Me too. They didn't expect such a turnout so they let one of the other girls go early. Crazy!"

"I've only been here once before, long time ago, and then it was pretty darn . . . " some man at a nearby table is trying to get the waitress's attention, waving his hand angrily.

"I'm sorry, can you hang on a minute?"

"Sure," Eddie says as she dashes away. He glances over to the bar and notices at once that the woman's gaze has left the bottom of her glass and now rests on him. Her eyes are shocking. A clear blue. Two small pieces of sky floating in the earthy brownness of her face. Eddie is overcome with embarrassment, as if it is not right that he be looking into those eyes.

"I'm sorry, this man just won't leave me alone! First it's the steak sauce, then the ice tea, now the topping on the cheesecake. I just can't believe some people."

Eddie looks at the waitress as if he's never seen her before. Then he remembers. "Halibut. Just gimme the fried halibut."

"Sure. Would you like a potato or rice?"

"Potato. And another drink."

"O.K, now what were you having?"

"What?"

"To drink."

"Oh. Soda. And scotch. I mean bourbon."

"Bourbon and soda?"

"Yeah."

"O.K, got it."

"Thanks." Eddie gives the girl a nod and looks down at the glass table top. In it he sees a muted image of himself. Unable to make out his features, he leans further down, the skin on his face falling slightly forward. Peeking out from behind enormous folds of skin, his eyes are little slits of nothingness, no color can be perceived. His lips appear blue, purple. The lips of his grandmother. Her hands were always so cold, as if she were only a few degrees away from death.

"Drop something?"

"Huh?"

"It looks like you dropped something." She sits down across from him.

"Oh, no. I just, yes, I just dropped this, this ring here."

"Not a wedding ring I hope." Her voice is low and soft and effortlessly appealing.

"Oh, no, no. Not me. You? I mean, are you married?"

"I saw you watching me over there." She pulls out a new cigarette and places it gently between her lips. She stares at Eddie, waiting for him to light it, until finally she picks up the matches from the clean ashtray and hands them to Eddie, watching him struggle to get one lit. "Thank you. Were you?"

"What?"

"Watching me."

"Well, I wouldn't say I was, uh, watching you, I think I did notice you a couple times." She smiles at Eddie, and he returns it gratefully. She takes a long drag on her cigarette and looks at Eddie, silently, not worrying about what she will say next.

"Do you, come here often?" The instant the words leave his mouth, Eddie puts his hand to his forehead and looks away. The woman doesn't blink. She only looks at him with her cool eyes.

"No. Do you?"

"No," Eddie says flatly, removing his hand and placing it on the table.

"Actually, I hate it here," she smiles.

"Really? Me, too. I really do. That's funny 'cause I thought you looked a little depressed over there. Would you like to tell me about it? Let me get you another drink. Miss? Miss? Aw hell, she should be over here pretty soon. What'll you have?"

"I really don't want another drink."

"Oh, O.K. Can I order you something else?"

"Well, seeing that we're both pretty unhappy here, it seems the best idea would be to leave."

Eddie catches his breath and forces a grin. "Actually, I was just waiting on some halibut. I haven't eaten a whole day. Wouldn't you rather just sit and . . . "

"How about if I make you a little something at my place?"

Eddie looks into the woman's eyes, but his gaze isn't confronted. He is traveling through her, drowning in her. Staring into her eyes is not like anything he has ever experienced. It lacks the usual human connection one experiences when looking into the eyes of another, the terrifying meeting with the person's soul. This gaze holds nothing for Eddie. It is empty.

"I'm just going to go to the restroom for a second." Eddie gets up carefully, without appearing too eager. "Don't go away, now."

Slowly, Eddie strides behind the bar and over to the waiters' station.

"Oh sir, I was just on my way with your drink."

"Don't worry about it. Here, this should cover it."

"But . . . oh. Thank you sir, very much. Come again now."

Eddie sees an exit at the back of the restaurant. He walks over to it and thrusts it open, so hard that it hits the outside wall. Not bothering to close the door, Eddie steps out into the night and breathes heavily. He takes a huge breath of air and as he holds it in, he looks up into the sky covered with stars. But the stars are not as clear as before. They appear hazy, and soon it looks to Eddie as if they have all merged into one single blanket of light, covering him. He lets the air out and coughs, gasping for another breath, but none will catch. The mistiness begins to solidify and huge tears well up in his eyes. Eddie sits down on the curb of the street, his hands pressing against his eyes, attempting to push the steady stream of liquid back into this head. The blanket of light above him has disappeared and all that is left is the night.

IF YOU WERE MY WOMAN

STEVE HAD ARRANGED TO PICK LENA UP at the salon where she worked at half-past two, and when he arrived she was out in front waiting, her leather backpack slung over one shoulder, her long chestnut hair just freshly washed and blown dry by expert hands. An hour and a half later they were already worlds away from the familiar L.A. streets, the shiny black Saab speeding across the Southern California desert like a spacecraft hurtling through the cosmos. It was like deep space out there in the desert, a vast emptiness which could make light speed look stationary, with only the rare cactus or rock or tumbleweed to mark one's forward motion.

Only an hour and a half into the trip and Steve had already checked the gas gauge seven times, anxious that he wouldn't find a service station when he needed one. There was still a good quarter of a tank left but when he saw the weathered wooden sign reading "Pete's Auto," he slammed his foot on the brake and swerved into the driveway.

Lena's long, bronzed arm shot up, bracing her against the dash board. She turned to Steve who smiled apologetically. "Sorry," he said, "but we need to get some gas." Lena hadn't felt how fast they were going until the sudden stop, when her stomach muscles tightened and her whole body shook as it settled into the strange new stillness. She remembered herself as a little girl driving with her mother, who would automatically extend her arm across her daughter's chest whenever the car made the slightest lunge, as if her white, fleshy limb could have protected Lena from harm. This time, Lena was glad she had been wearing her seat belt.

It was the first stop on their weekend trip and Lena tried to hide her pleasure at finding such a picturesque filling station, like something you might find on an old Hollywood back lot. It was too perfect to be real. She was aching to get out of the car and feel the soft, dusty earth under her boots. "I'll fill her up," she said, holding out her hand. Steve shrugged and gave her the keys.

Lena didn't see anyone around. She figured this wasn't a pay before you pump sort of place, so she went ahead and unlocked the gas tank. She pulled the heavy nozzle over to the back of the car with one arm, inserted it into the metal hole, and squeezed the lever with an even, firm grip while her other arm rested lithely against her side. She wore a red cropped tank top and stiff, tight blue jeans which accentuated her long legs. She liked how her hair felt against the bare skin of her shoulders, the fat curls which Yvonne had made with the help of a strong-holding mousse and a hot iron. She wore little make-up because it was summer and her face glowed golden from weekends on the beach. Just a little black liner around the eyes which the girls at the shop said made her look like an Egyptian queen. Lena could see herself at that moment, from way up high, standing there tall and striking against the black mirrored surface of the car, the wind blowing her hair, the red dust swirling around her legs. She thought she must look like one of those models on television, advertising cars or domestic beer, an apparition of loveliness in the midst of decaying life.

When the tank was full, Lena replaced the nozzle and headed towards the office, in search of someone to pay.

"I hope you got cash, Miss. Cause we don't take no credit." Against the paint-stripped outside wall of the office sat a middle-aged man with a Goodyear hat on his head and a cigarette hanging out of his mouth. Lena wondered if he'd been sitting there against the wall all along, watching as she stood filling the tank, as she walked confidently over to the office with her long-legged stride.

"I think I have some cash," Lena said, trying to smile, and when the man smiled back she noticed he was missing more teeth than she could count.

"You didn't happen to notice how much gas you pumped."

Yes, she had remembered. "Fourteen dollars and eighty cents."

As she jammed her hands into the stiff denim, hoping she hadn't forgotten to stuff her tips into her pockets before she left, Lena noticed the man staring beyond her, at the car, and she figured he was looking at Steve. The man stared in a way which seemed unusual for him, although how Lena knew what was usual or unusual for this toothless gas station owner she wasn't quite sure. Yet he stared with such intensity, Lena could not resist turning around and looking for herself.

There Steve sat, looking straight ahead, still wearing his dark sunglasses, not once turning towards the office where Lena stood talking to the man who must certainly have been Pete.

"If you were my woman," Pete said, and Lena abruptly turned her head back to face him, "you wouldn't be pumpin' any gas. And you sure wouldn't be payin' for it." At that moment Lena pulled out two ten dollar bills from her pocket, sweaty and wilted from hours tucked within the thick hot denim of her jeans. She handed the limp, slightly soggy bills to Pete, feeling like she was giving him something too intimate, a part of herself he did not yet deserve.

Pete took the bills and held them, looking at them and letting them rest in his palms, as if he too felt the transaction to be overly familiar. Then he looked up and said, "I'll get you some change." He got up out of his chair and went inside the office. Lena took the opportunity to look back at Steve, hoping he had found reason enough to look her way. But there he was, still facing straight ahead, waiting patiently for Lena's inevitable return.

"Hope that'll do ya," said Pete as he handed Lena a five dollar bill. "I'm low on change."

"Of course, no problem," and Lena smiled wide, as if it were he that had done her the favor.

Steve had taken Lena to many places during their eight month relationship, but never to the exclusive spa which sat like an oasis in the middle of the Mojave Desert. He used to bring other girl friends there, especially his last, Genie, who everyone at the spa had known by name. Lena had gotten it into her head that it was important for Steve to bring her to that particular place, that it would somehow prove something, and finally, after much cajoling, he gave in.

As Steve checked-in at the blue and white tiled desk at the front of the lobby, Lena kept herself at a distance, waiting with their luggage a good ten feet away. Every once in a while the woman behind the desk would look up from her paperwork and steal a glance at Lena, then quickly look away. Lena thought that maybe the woman was surprised to see Steve there without Genie, with another woman instead. Or maybe she thought that Lena was Genie, only different. A new hair-do, a little less heavy around the rear. Or maybe there wasn't much difference between her and Genie at all.

A young man came and collected their luggage, but Lena insisted on carrying her backpack. Steve allowed the rather slight young man to carry all of his things, even his briefcase which he brought with him everywhere. He walked through the open, cloistered corridors along the garden with his arms swinging freely, and Lena wondered why he hadn't offered to carry her bag. Lena thought that the young man wondered the same thing, because when he showed them into their room he gave Lena an odd look, a look she had recognized from earlier that day.

Steve had warned Lena that dinner was a rather formal occasion at the spa, so she had come prepared with a brand new dress for both nights. She had thought that she'd save the silver sheath dress cut low in the back for Saturday evening, but when she opened her hanging bag and saw the delicate fabric shimmer from behind dry cleaner's plastic, she couldn't resist the idea of starting the weekend off the best way possible.

When she stepped cautiously into the dining room with her silver spiked heels and sheer hose sprinkled with glitter, a familiar wave of embarrassment overtook Lena, and she felt as if maybe she had tried too hard to look beautiful, that perhaps everyone could easily gauge the amount of effort she had put into her appearance that evening. But the admiring looks of the maitre-d, the waiters, and the other men who stood by the door waiting for their tables, assured her that no such censure was taking place.

Lena liked being looked at, enjoyed the bold eye contact that a handsome man would venture when she walked into a room, but tonight it seemed the looks were all too abrupt. She watched those men with tanned faces and slicked back hair look at her, their eyes running from head to foot, but then their glances quickly shifted to Steve who remained oblivious to the attention. How long will a person admire a sports car, a yacht, a sprawling estate, before his eye wanders in search of an owner? Suddenly a wave of heat spread across Lena's bare shoulders, and it rose until she could feel it burning her cheeks, her mouth becoming dry and parched. She thought of the swimming pool sitting in the court-yard. She wanted to jump in, heels and all, and sizzle like a steak doused in wine. But before she could move the maitre-d appeared and took her hand, and as they walked through the dim velvet of the dining room, a slight breeze brushed across Lena's scantily cov-ered body, making her shiver.

The room was dark when they came back well after mid-night, so Lena couldn't see the wicker settee, the Mexican rugs, the red tiled floors. All she saw was blackness when Steve took hold of her waist and started kissing her neck, and the feeling was so foreign that she realized it was the first time he'd touched her all day. He kissed her neck and her shoulders, then moved up to her mouth, forcing her lips apart with his tongue, sucking on her moistness like a man dying of thirst. His hands went up her dress and she could feel him looking for a zipper, but there wasn't one. It had taken Lena five minutes to squeeze into this three hundred dollar dress, and she didn't think Steve would be willing to wait that long for her to get out of it.

He lifted her arms and began yanking it up, over her shoulders, over her head, catching her hair in the fabric and pulling it as he struggled with the unyielding material. He stopped when he saw her tight stomach encased in nylon, her braless breasts exposed, and he kissed her torso as her arms remained tangled, her head covered, the dress pressed against her mouth and nose, making it difficult to breath. She was still struggling with the dress when he pushed her onto the bed and pulled off her stockings. And he was already inside of her before she could finally pick the silver threads out of her mouth and take a breath of air.

Before she could even think, he was inside her, before she could decide if it was what she wanted. It wasn't, she thought, but how could she tell him that now? She didn't have a good enough reason to make him stop, a reason good enough to avoid a fight, avoid him being annoyed with her and suggesting an early departure. He was almost finished anyway, she could tell by the pinched grimace on his face, and soon enough it would be over.

He lay beside her, still breathing hard and fast, his eyes closed, so he didn't notice when she got up and stood next to the bed. The room was heavy with the smell of sweat and sex and Lena felt sick to her stomach. She walked slowly toward the bathroom and turned on the light, but was immediately repelled by the antiseptic white tiles and her ghostlike reflection in the mirror. So she headed for the door.

The French doors at the back of the room opened up onto nothing—no pool, no jacuzzi, no pebbled paths, no flowers or plants or trees which needed constant attention—only desert. Once outside Lena took a deep breath, and the clean, dry air, the desert air which is void of the scents of life, soothed her, making her legs buckle, her body drop to the ground.

Only when she felt the earth beneath her, a sharp edged stone pressing into her thigh, did she realize she was still naked. She leaned over, onto her side, her arm tucked beneath her, her legs bent and parted like a Chinese fan, the side of her face resting in a flat, stoneless spot of earth. As she lay there feeling the dirt against her skin, she thought of the many pictures she'd seen, of women, beautiful women, sprawled on the beach, grains of golden sand stuck to their ocean-soaked bodies, their backs arched, faces lifted up towards the sun. Lena felt nothing like those women. There in the desert it was dark and there was no ocean, no water in sight. Her body was dry, except for a few drops of semen which still clung to the insides of her thighs, attracting the rough, dusty dirt which was nothing like sand. Her body wasn't spread in a flattering pose. Her shoulders were hunched, her stomach folded into thin rolls of fat, and her breasts hung to the side, two sagging triangles of flesh. But Lena didn't care. She didn't want to look like anything just then. She wanted only to sleep.

Lena woke at dawn, the sun appearing suddenly like a ripe tropical fruit. She opened her eyes but didn't move, just squinted into the sun and watched as it went from a serene red to a blazing yellow, as if that mature piece of fruit were gradually becoming younger over time. Lena also felt younger at that moment, like a child awake before the rest of the family, alone with the mysteries of the morning. She couldn't remember ever being so dirty, not since she was a little girl, making mud pies in her back yard.

After a while the sun became hotter, and Lena knew it meant that soon, others would be rising. They would drink their coffee, take their showers, dress for the day. Then she noticed the line of French doors on either side of her, doors to other rooms, with people inside. She wondered if they might come out for a breath of air, a look at the sun, the desert. Then they might see her there, lying naked in the dirt, and they would think she was sick or dead and go running for the hotel manager. But Lena was confident that wouldn't happen. She was sure that no one could see her, for she was in the process of becoming invisible.

RESULTS

IT WAS TUESDAY AND NELL WAS STAYING HOME from work. She set her alarm for 6:00 A.M. so she could leave a message on her supervisor's voice mail before he got in. She figured her voice would automatically sound sick at six in the morning. Nell really didn't feel well, but, most of all, today was the day she'd be getting back her results.

She climbed back in bed and lay awake for an hour until Paul got up at 7:00. He kissed her good morning and then grabbed his towel and went into the bathroom. Nell was glad he hadn't asked her why she was still in bed. He must have remembered her telling him that she'd be staying home today.

She listened to the buzz of his electric razor, then the shower, then the hair dryer. She heard the bathroom door open and then footsteps to the kitchen. She lay there, eyes staring at the ceiling, and heard the steamy swishing of the coffee maker, the opening of the refrigerator, the clicking of spoon against mug. With each new sound, each creak, knock and click, Nell could feel her body rise involuntarily, towards the action, but she just kept reminding herself that today was different.

"Good-bye," said Paul and he kissed Nell on the cheek.

"Bye," she said. "Have a good day."

Paul stood and looked at Nell longer than he would have normally. For a brief moment his eyelids became heavy and his mouth
started to twitch. He felt it and quickly forced a smile. "You, too,"
he said.

Once she heard the front door slam and the dead bolt turn,
Nell allowed herself to get out of bed. She had waited till Paul was
out of the house, so she would be free to wander aimlessly, or stand
and stare out the window, or even just lean against a wall.

Nell went into the kitchen and decided to have tea instead of
coffee today. She toasted a piece of wheat bread and buttered it
well. Then, on a whim, she sprinkled some cinnamon and sugar on
top. She hadn't done that in a long time. She sat, drinking her tea
and eating her toast, wondering what she'd be doing next.

At ten o'clock she could make phone calls, but it was still only
8:30. She decided to turn on the television. She had hoped to wait
awhile longer before resorting to the TV, but then she figured she
didn't really have to leave it on. She could turn it off and turn it on
according to how she felt. And besides, nobody had to know.

The morning news show was still on. The digital clock was running along in the corner, 8:34, 8:35, 8:36. Nell didn't appreciate
having that constant reminder of time passing, but she figured she
could handle it until 9:00 when the show was over. A movie actress
was on plugging her new film. Nell recognized the actress, even
knew her name. She wished she didn't. But whether she liked it or
not, Nell knew the actress's name and would probably never forget
it. All she could do was decide not to go see her new film, in
protest.

Nell turned off the television promptly at 9:00, not wanting to
see what the next offering would be, avoiding the possibility of getting hooked. She went to her desk and noted the clock, 9:01. She
took out her calendar and opened up to today, Tuesday. One entry.
The following days were completely empty, empty through the next
three months, up until Paul's birthday. Then came Christmas, but
Nell didn't have to fill anything in there. The calendar people had
already done that for her. She wondered if she had put her mother's
birthday in yet. She flipped to March and saw that it too was

empty. She figured she'd take this opportunity to fill in the birth-days of her parents and two sisters. She couldn't remember exactly when her friend Sally's birthday was, but she knew it was either April 4 or 6. She'd have to find that out.

Before she knew it, it was 10:00. Now she could start making phone calls. She picked up the phone and was about to dial her sis-ter's number when she quickly hung up. Actually, she didn't really want to talk to anyone today. They'd just ask what she was doing home and she really didn't want to talk about it. Besides, if the office called it might not look so good if the line was busy for too long. She decided she'd take a shower.

The hot water felt good running down her back. It made her sleepy. She sat down in the tub, and found the water felt different down there. The droplets must have gathered a great deal of momentum during their lengthy fall, causing them to crash down on Nell's head in a thumping, haphazard way. Sitting down there in the tub, Nell had an idea. Why not take a bath? She pushed down the shower button and flicked the metal lever which would stop up the tub. The warm water filled the spaces around her and she lay back against the white porcelain edge.

Steam came pouring out into the hall when she finally opened the bathroom door. She stumbled a bit, dizzy and light-headed. She couldn't believe her eyes when she saw that it was already 11:12. That made her feel even dizzier. She lay down on the bed, wrapped tightly in a towel, and rested. She still felt hot, so she loosened the towel and pushed it down to her waist. Now the cool air covered her arms and chest and she could feel the blood going back into her head. She opened her eyes, looked at the ceiling, then closed them again.

She rose at 11:53 and wrapped the towel around her so that it covered her breasts. She went to her dresser and opened the top drawer, pulling out a pair of cotton underwear and some thick white socks. After she dressed, she went back to the bathroom and blew her hair dry. She made no attempt to style it as she usually did, just blew it straight. She didn't mind the way it looked when she had finished. Maybe she'd wear her hair this way from now on.

When she finally reached the kitchen once again, it was 12:32, time for lunch. She opened a can of tuna, drained out the water, and plopped it into a stainless steel mixing bowl. She added a substantial spoonful of mayonnaise, some Dijon mustard, pickle relish, lemon juice, salt, pepper, and a dash of paprika. She had always liked paprika and wondered why she didn't use it more often. She took out an onion and sliced off a piece, chopping it finely into neat little squares. She added in the onion and gave the whole thing a final stir. Then she scooped the mixture onto two slices of wheat bread, and carefully laid a slice of American cheese on each. She put the open-faced sandwiches in the toaster oven and watched as they turned brown. She then cut two slices of tomato and placed them on top of the soft, warm cheese. She put it all on a plate, poured herself a glass of orange juice and went back into the living room and turned on the TV.

A soap opera was just starting, the one she used to watch as a teenager. She was mildly interested in seeing how the show's characters were doing. Many of the same characters she remembered were still on the show. The stately matriarch with the elaborate hairdo which relied much too heavily on hair spray. The philandering father with the carefully placed grey around the temples. And so many good-looking young men and women. Nell wondered where they all came from, all these perky blonde-haired women with huge, round, blue eyes, and the slinky brunettes with almond-shaped brown eyes peeking out from behind thick, wavy tresses. And the men, so tall and sleek with broad shoulders and longish straight hair. They all looked so healthy and vibrant, so active and full of purpose. Of course their lives were full of problems and danger, but somehow it seemed a small price to pay for feeling so alive.

They kept calling this one woman Jenny, but she didn't look like the Jenny that Nell had remembered. This Jenny had red hair. Didn't she used to be blonde? They must have replaced the old Jenny, thought Nell. Maybe she was getting too old, or maybe she's gone onto bigger and better things, like the movies, only Nell couldn't remember having seen her in anything. Or maybe she had to quit the show for health reasons. Maybe she had received some bad results.

The phone rang. The warm, tangy cheese and soft, creamy tuna which had tasted so good to Nell before suddenly became watery and stale. The phone rang again but Nell couldn't seem to chew anymore, to swallow. She went to her desk and grabbed a tissue, spitting out the half-chewed mass. She wiped her mouth with another tissue, but couldn't rid herself of the strange, metallic after-taste.

"Hello," she said, still struggling to swallow the remnants of the tuna.

"How ya doing?" asked Paul.

The tiny slivers of tuna finally went down. "Fine," Nell said. She swallowed again. "How are you?"

"O.K. Tired. I wish I could've stayed home today."

"No you don't."

There was silence on the other end. Paul wished he hadn't said what he did. Nell knew it, so she went on. "Work's going bad?"

"No, not really. I would've liked to stay home with you, that's all."

"I know," said Nell. She could hear the soap opera continue in the other room.

"What're ya doin'?"

"Eating lunch."

"What're ya eatin'?"

"Tuna."

"Hmmm. I think I'll go get a slice of pizza."

"That sounds good."

"Well, I just wanted to see how you were."

"They haven't called yet, Paul."

"I know. I just wanted to say hi."

"I know. I'm just telling you."

"O.K. I guess I'll go to lunch now."

"O.K., bye."

"Bye."

Nell hung up the phone and leaned back in her chair. She looked at the clock on her desk and it read 1:47. She wondered if it was too early to call.

"Nell, Nell Williams," said Nell.

"No, I'm sorry, Ms. Williams. We haven't got those results in yet. They should be coming sometime after 4:00," said the nurse.

"O.K., I'll try again later."

And Nell hung up the phone. She sat at her desk, in silence, till the clock changed to 2:00, and then got up. She decided to make herself another cup of tea.

On top of the refrigerator was a magazine. It must have been there for a long time because the pages were warped and a little damp. But what really gave away its age was the date in the top right hand corner. It was one of those city magazines, its title borrowed directly from the name of the town about which it spoke. It was full of features on well-known, accomplished citizens of the city, listings of all the city's cultural events, open markets and fairs, and advertisements for local shops and restaurants. From the looks of that magazine, Nell's home was quite a busy, cosmopolitan place, with much more to offer its residents than one might think. Nell had always meant to circle the places and happenings which interested her, or cut them out and tape them to the refrigerator. But she never did. She wondered whether now was the time to start. At that moment, Nell understood that she might soon have to make a choice. She started to think about all the many made-for-TV-movies she had seen, movies about cancer patients or women with multiple sclerosis or little autistic boys. Everyone seemed so brave in those movies, had chosen to accept what time and what strength they were given and make the most of their lives. Nell wondered what she would do in a similar situation. But now was not the time to make that choice. She would wait, wait until she had to.

Nell added lots of milk and honey to her cup of tea. She even sprinkled a little cinnamon on top. She wished she had some sort of cookie to have with it. She even considered making some cookies, snickerdoodles or some such sugar cookie. But finally, she decided against it. She sat at the kitchen table, the TV still going in the other room, and drank her tea.

She went back into the living room and started watching a talk show which was just coming on. Mother-daughter pairs sat up on the stage. All the mothers had, at one time or another, slept with their daughters' boyfriends. They were all so courageous, these mothers and daughters, talking openly and freely about what must have been a very painful subject in their lives. Some of them even laughed, mostly when the audience burst out in laughter.

There was one girl, though, who didn't laugh. In fact, she looked like she might start crying at any minute. It seemed she really loved this boyfriend of hers and had been going out with him for maybe five years. He had said more than once that he loved her, too. Then one day she came home to find him and her mother in the shower together. The girl was mad at her boyfriend, of course. Still hadn't forgiven him. But her mother. How could her mother do that to her? the girl asked the audience. Maybe they had some clue. The mother just sat there. Maybe she too was hoping the audience would be able to tell her what had possessed her to call the girl's boyfriend into the bathroom and coax him into the shower with her. It seemed so unnecessary to the daughter. She understood that her mother liked the idea of doing something she wasn't supposed to do, but she wondered why her mother couldn't have picked something that wouldn't have hurt so badly.

Nell wondered the same thing. But then, people hurt each other all the time, for no good reason. It's too bad, thought Nell. Enough bad things happen all on their own without people actually doing something to cause them to happen.

Nell wasn't sure how long she could listen to these stories. Although, she had to admit, she was pretty interested in all the crazy ways these mom's managed to seduce their daughters' boyfriends. She wasn't proud of it, but she was curious about all that sleaze.

At the commercial break, the hostess announced tomorrow's subject, hermaphrodites. Nell doubted that most of the viewing audience even knew what that meant. She was glad to be going back to work tomorrow so that she wouldn't have to watch that show. But then, what if the results weren't back yet? She might have to stay home again tomorrow. She figured she'd be able to find some other program to watch.

Then a thought crossed her mind. What if the results came back and everything was fine? Then what? Wouldn't there be more results to wait for soon enough? Wouldn't there always be some sort of results to wait for? Whether people know it or not, they're always waiting for results. Nell felt as if she knew something that everybody else didn't. Then she wondered if she had enough money saved to stay home everyday and wait for results.

When the show was finally over, it was 4:00. Nell waited as long as she could before she actually called. She didn't want to have to call again if the results still hadn't arrived.

"Hi, this is Nell Williams."

"Can you hold a moment, please."

Nell waited. She wondered if it wouldn't have been a better idea to have gone to work today after all. She considered hanging up and driving to work and calling again from there. Or maybe she could go to Paul's office. Suddenly, she worried about being by herself. How could Paul have left her alone like this?

"Hello?"

"Yes, this is Nell Williams."

"Yes?"

"I'm calling to check on my results. They were due in today."

"Let's see here. Oh, yes, Ms. Williams. Yes. Your results just came in."

"Uh, huh."

"Everything's fine, Ms. Williams. No abnormalities."

"It was fine? I mean, that's it?"

"That's it," said the nurse.

Nell could almost hear the nurse's smile. "Thank you."

"Now I need to make another appointment for you in about six months."

"What for?"

"The doctor would like to perform more tests then, just to make sure everything remains normal."

"Why?"

"This is just standard procedure, Ms. Williams. Let's see, how's January 12th, at 11:00 in the morning?"

Nell opened her calendar. January was wide open. "That's fine."

"We'll see you then."

"All right," said Nell and she hung up the phone.

She wrote down the appointment in her calendar. Then she flipped back through all of the blank pages which preceded January 12th and wondered if at some point, they might be filled in.

UP AND DOWN

It's your sciatic nerve."

I put my hand to my lower back once again. Now I had something to look for.

"I wasn't even doing anything strenuous. Just bent over and all of a sudden this pain shoots down my back into my legs."

"Sciatic nerve," Wendy said as she straightened her helmet, finally putting an end to this mystery. She didn't really want to hear anymore about it. She knew what it was. Now I did. Let's get on with it.

And I knew just when to keep quiet. I pulled down my cap, tucked my hair behind my ears, and followed Wendy's lead.

"My mother had the same thing," Wendy said without looking back.

I knew that other women my age found perverse pleasure in bemoaning the fact that they were "becoming their mothers," but I was never particularly disturbed by the character traits I possessed which some might describe as maternal. I like to cook and I like people to eat my cooking. One of my worst nightmares is that someone will leave my table hungry. Having a back problem is another story.

"Face it, Jane, we're getting old!" said Wendy as she swerved her front wheel to the left, avoiding a sharp rock sitting maliciously in her path. Her legs started pumping faster, perfectly in synch with her studied breathing, as if what she were really saying was that *I* was getting older, while *she* was doing everything she could to keep herself young and healthy, and doing a fine job of it.

I watched as Wendy rode her way steadily up the incline, her fluorescent pink and green lycra jump suit gleaming in the hot sun. She always had the right equipment. The special shoes with the little holes in the sole which fit right onto the pedals of her eighteen-hundred-dollar mountain bike. She read tons of mountain biking magazines before deciding on that bike. Wendy always seemed to be completely informed about every activity in which she decided to participate. I wondered how she managed to find the time.

I, on the other hand, didn't have the right equipment. There I was on some barren, rocky mountain with tires half the diameter of Wendy's, cut off sweat pants, Ked's tennis shoes, and a purple cotton baseball hat, hardly the kind of protection my cranium needed from the blow to my head which was sure to accompany my inevitable wipe out.

Trying to mimic Wendy's expert breathing, I pushed my feet against the pedals with all my might, but the wheel simply wouldn't turn. For a moment, the bike stood motionless, and I, perched on top, held my breath, waiting for the bike to start tipping to the side. But it didn't. It seemed as if the bike had no intention of falling over in the least and was determined to just wait for me to begin pedaling again. So I got off the bike.

"I'm gonna have to walk up this one," I shouted up to Wendy when she turned around and saw me demount. She just kept pedaling on.

"Meet you at the top."

So what if I'm getting old. I've lived a full life. Sometimes I find myself taking stock of my life, a sort of temporal inventory giving me the evidence I need to determine whether I have been living my life wisely and successfully. Four years of college. That's good. Got a good education, solid liberal arts background. Didn't go to grad school, but then that probably would have been too much. A waste of time. A few trips to Europe. My affair with Pierre in Paris. I rack up a lot of points for that one. A month-long affair with a Frenchman in Paris. Cafés, nightclubs, strolls on the Seine and all. I could have quit after that and would have been O.K. But I didn't quit.

I could barely see Wendy. Not wanting to get too far behind, I quickly hopped back onto my bike, invigorated by the secure knowledge that I had lived a good, full life, thereby making the conquering of this mere hill inconsequential. As I pushed in vain, I wondered whether my pitiful showing was on account of my poor equipment or my utter lack of strength and perseverance. I started picturing those sweaty women in the running shoe ads who soared to the mountain's precipice, seemingly on the strength of their own sheer will. Perhaps, if I could only imagine reaching the top, I would, but my mind kept going back to the dismount that seemed to have already taken place, making my efforts as futile as resuscitating a dead man.

Pushing the bike up that forty-five degree incline wasn't really much easier. What had appeared as a glorious, commanding presence from the grassy knoll below, became suddenly sinister only minutes after the climb began. This arid mound of dirt, void of any life, void of the moisture of which life is made, would eventually spell my doom. It cradled me in its worn, jagged path, lifting me high above all that was in sight, all else in the world, offering me to the sun like a sacrifice. I hung my head down, sweat pouring into my eyes, the earth below me a terra-cotta blur, when suddenly, I was startled by Wendy's voice.

"Isn't this great?" she said with a smile, looking around her with serene awe.

I had reached the top. In order to satisfy Wendy I immediately took a quick look around me and nodded. I then took off my hat and wiped my forehead with my sleeve.

Wendy pulled a water bottle from the frame of her bike and held it a good six inches from her mouth, squirting the steady stream straight down her throat. No need to pass the water along her tongue, to feel the dampness in her parched mouth. The danger of dehydration was all too near. She pulled out a wheat germ, apricot power bar, sat down on the edge of the cliff, and began eating as she gazed out over the blue ocean.

I was still breathing heavily, nowhere near recovered from the push I had just performed. I pulled an old plastic mineral water bottle out of my back pack, and sucked out a mouthful of the tap water with which I had filled it that morning. My nose unable to intake enough air, I was forced to open my mouth, letting the remaining water slide out the corners.

"God, would you look at this, Jane?"

But I could not. My eyes stung from the sweat of my efforts and I was no more interested in looking out over the ocean, watching its blueness shimmer against the earthen tones of the rocky cliffs, then I was in continuing on with this perilous excursion.

What had happened to me? I wondered. Was there not a time when such a magnificent vision would enchant me, when I would rise to the challenge of an athletic risk? My mind drifted to almost three years earlier, my last trip to Europe.

I had been in Rome only a month, and a friend had given me his old bicycle to use. It was in such bad shape it could barely hold my weight, so I wheeled it over to Piazza Navona, where a strange little bike shop sat, plopped in the midst of elegant, marble-filled cafés and rows of pink cotton tablecloths. While mustachioed waiters in white jackets served espresso and multicolored liqueurs to their beautiful and/or rich patrons, a white-haired man in blue grease-covered overalls was fixing bikes. There were a couple of racing bikes hanging on the huge wooden door which opened up onto the piazza, and the thick tire of a lone mountain bike peeped out from the darkness within, but it was clear that this mechanic specialized in hopeless cases.

I wheeled my bike in front of the old man's shop, sure that this would be the one he'd have nothing to do with. He was fixing another bike as I waited, similar to mine, with it's flimsy black wheel protectors and deflated old tires, which hugged the craggy cobblestones under the slightest bit of pressure. There were no tools in his wrinkled old hands. He worked fast, pushing and pulling at the bike's parts, which seemed to be all too few. I looked down at my bike for a moment. That was it! It seemed to be missing parts. But which ones? I looked back up and the man was already handing the bike back to its owner.

When he finished with my bike, I took out my wallet and asked him how much I owed him. He grimaced and waved his hand, as if payment were not expected. *"Dieci?"* I asked and held out a ten thousand lira bill. He shook his head and held up two fingers. I smiled big and then waved as I rode away, feeling that my thank you was embarrassingly insufficient. The man's countenance remained the same, his mouth pursed shut and his eyes turned down at the corners. My wave became more excited as I swung around the piazza, back towards the shop. The old man looked up at me and blessed me with a nod, lowering his head only a fraction, then raising it high, looking out and over, beyond me, commanding me to move on.

I rode down one of the narrow streets which ran perpendicular to the piazza. The smooth motion of the pedals belied the erratic bumping beneath me. This bike would carry me through anything, unfazed by whatever might threaten its forward motion.

At the end of one winding street there was always another, more narrow, more foreboding. But with each turn of the wheel, I conquered them all. If the bright white headlights of an oncoming car hadn't met me out of nowhere, I never would have realized that night had fallen. Suddenly I was lost. But before I could ponder my predicament, before the slightest bit of worry could invade my mind, I turned out of the dark alleyway onto a magnificent boulevard. Night became evening and the reds and purples of the previously hidden sky greeted me and pointed me in the right direction.

As I glided down the perfectly paved road, I smiled up into the sky. I knew where I was. Any minute now I'd see those ancient stones, the ones that withstood Nero's water, that contained the roars of lions, that entombed the mightiest of warriors.

The strips of color weaved in and out of those massive arches and all I could think was that they wouldn't stay there for long. In an instant the pattern would unravel like a loose braid and the voids would be filled with a rich, solid blue. I didn't slow down to watch, but sped on by, knowing that every image that followed would be as striking as this one.

Ground that I had once trod on like an ordinary human was now traversed by some other type of being. No longer a part of the ground below me or the air around me, I was utterly alone.

This was before Paris, before Pierre, before strolls on the Seine, my hand tucked safely inside his. Before seeing things through the eyes of another, myself through the eyes of another.

Maybe I had quit after Paris. What had that lousy Frenchman done to me? I had once suggested we rent bikes and ride out into the countryside and pick strawberries, but Pierre only guffawed and quickly whisked me off to a nearby Brasserie for beer and french fries. I stayed an extra three weeks in Paris, loathe to part with my newfound companion. And once I returned to the states, it was as if I had permanently lost a part of myself.

I waited until Wendy finished her power bar and then asked nonchalantly, "You want to get going?"

Wendy was clearly annoyed, or maybe more surprised than anything else. She got up and mounted her bike. Without so much as a word or a glance, Wendy headed downhill.

It seemed to be the cruelest of jokes. There I was, standing at this presumed summit, having survived if not conquered this pitiful hill which had been so determined to sink me, looking down into a deadly sea of rocks and cracks. Suddenly, it became clear that there would never be any rest.

I got on my bike and started down.

"It's actually easier if you go a little faster!" Wendy shouted up at me. I squeezed my brakes harder as I inched my way down.

My hands turned red and the sweat which poured from my palms made it impossible to hold on any longer. I either had to get off, or let go. Before a decision could be made, my hands slipped off the metal and the bike went speeding forth.

I didn't look up from the ground as I tried to replace my hands on the brakes and maintain a grip. All I could do was close my eyes to the cloud of dirt that rose and encompassed me. The only thing greater than my fear was the bewilderment I felt as I passed over ground that for some reason was sparing me.

I could hear the echo of Wendy's joyous yelps as she zoomed down, faster and faster, staring straight ahead, at the sea which she was bound to reach.

I might have been going at a velocity which rivaled Wendy's, but in my mind, I was doing nothing but falling. I was falling right, and falling left. I was hitting a rock head on, flying over the handle bars, impaling myself on my kickstand.

It seems all I do anymore is fall. Never looking up at the peak whence I came, nor for a handhold which could possibly save me.

SWEET TOOTH

ONE EGGS AND SAUSAGE AND ONE FRENCH TOAST." The waitress set the steaming hot plates down in front of us. "Enjoy."

"Grazie, Bella," said Johnny with a wink.

Anywhere else in the city, Johnny's flirting would have made me jealous. But here we were in Little Italy, Johnny's homeland. I didn't want to repress his old world instincts.

"Mmm, the sausage is excellent today. Try some." Johnny held out his fork with a piece of crumpled, yellow flecked meat hanging on precariously.

"I'd rather not."

"C'mon, it's good!"

"I'm sure it is, I just don't want any. Thanks." I'd considered becoming a vegetarian simply to avoid such moments, but it seemed kind of a cop-out. Besides, I liked chicken.

"Well, I don't know how you can eat all that sugar and syrup first thing in the morning," said Johnny as he stuck the already chilled chunk of sausage in his mouth with an air of defeat.

I felt bad. He had just wanted me to experience the same kind of pleasure he was experiencing with his grease-covered sausage smeared with yolk. But what could I do? The fact was that Johnny preferred savory and I preferred sweet. I had already accepted that and I only wished that Johnny would do the same.

As we got up to leave the restaurant I could see Johnny's eyes dart around, looking for our waitress. He didn't like to leave without saying good-bye.

"Bye, Jane!" said Johnny.

"Bye, Johnny," said the waitress. Then she looked at me and awkwardly said, "Bye."

I didn't really mind that no one in the neighborhood bothered to learn my name. At least they smiled. I guess they must have known that I wasn't Italian. They'd have figured that with my blond hair, pale blue eyes, and turned-up nose, I was of Nordic descent. But the truth was that no one in my family had any idea where our ancestors came from. It was as if the neighborhood knew that I had never lived in a community of my own, that I had never walked down the street, greeted by shop owners and street vendors as I passed. They probably just didn't want to shock me.

"Shoot!"

"What?" Johnny stopped in his tracks and looked at me with concern.

"Oh, I just forgot to get quarters." We were already half-way to our doorstep.

Johnny looked behind him, at the long block we had just traversed. "Can you just get them when you come down?"

"With all the laundry?"

"You can load the stuff in first and then go get quarters."

I didn't know what I wanted him to say. I didn't want to turn back and retrace our steps any more than he did. "O.K.," I said.

I went into the laundry and loaded up three washers. The quarter machine, with its pitiful "out of order" sign masking some fatal, mechanical flaw, stared at me and I stared back with disdain. I went to the doorway, then looked back at the three washers I had filled. I hoped that no one would come and steal our clothes. But then I figured that if anyone was so bad-off that they had to steal somebody's dirty laundry, maybe it was all for the best.

I was determined not to take the long trek down the block, back to our "commercial center." There had to be something closer by. A couple doors down was the antique hat shop. The sign said it would be open from 2:00 to 6:00 today. Supposedly, this place was to be open everyday from 2:00 to 6:00, a rather short period of time in which to catch a person while in the midst of a crazy urge to buy an antique hat. If you asked me, the less useful the product, the longer the hours had to be. But they wouldn't have any quarters anyway. I'd have bet that a quarter hadn't passed that store's threshold since the day it opened.

Up ahead I could see red and blue neon lights lit up in a huge storefront window. Could it be the liquor store was open? Weren't there laws about liquor being sold on Sunday, or was that only in mid-western states whose republican senators had ruled since the Revolution? As I walked into the warm, wine-filled store, I was glad to be living in a democratic majority.

"Hi," I said. I was happy and in no hurry to fill my hands full of quarters. I'd make a little small talk first.

"Can I help you?" It seemed this guy didn't really want to be open this Sunday morning.

"Could you change a few singles for some quarters?"

The guy shamelessly rolled his eyes and opened the cash register drawer. He poked his finger through a rather shallow pool of change. "I can't spare any."

"None?" I asked.

The guy looked back down. "O.K., I'll give you four."

I handed the guy a dollar bill and took the four quarters. A lot of good that would do me. "Thank you," I said, with a little too much enthusiasm. I think the guy got the point.

I walked over to the sunny side of the street and continued down the block. I knew there'd be nothing open, but I kept going anyway. Past the Italian restaurant, the leather repair shop. By that time, I could have been to the commercial center and back already, my pockets full of the quarters which Jane the waitress would have so graciously given me.

And then, there it was. An old wooden door propped open, exposing another glass door with a "Yes, We're Open" sign hanging proudly in the center. Behind the door I could see a small, simulated wood-paneled room with a long bar lined with red vinyl standing towards the back. On top of the bar sat a shiny new espresso machine, a piece of plastic still wrapped around the spout for the steam.

I hadn't remembered ever seeing this place. I looked again at the old wooden door and realized that I had seen it before, only then it had been just a closed door with "Da Mauro" scrawled over the top. I looked inside again and over against the wall sat what appeared to be "Mauro," an old, round, balding man with a short black mustache. I was disappointed not to see even a trace of a cash register.

"Excuse me," I said. Even though this was clearly a place of business, I couldn't help feeling I was intruding.

Mauro looked at me but didn't smile. I wondered why he wasn't happier to see me.

I looked at the espresso machine, wishing from the bottom of my heart that I drank coffee.

"The machine does not work yet!" Mauro shouted at me. "I can give you a soda!"

"Well, actually, I just wanted to see if perhaps, maybe, you might have some quarters to spare." I waited in terror for Mauro to strike.

"Quarters!" he said. "You want quarters?" All of a sudden, Mauro's face broke out into a smile. The fact that I had no intention of actually patronizing this business of his seemed to suddenly warm him up to me. Mauro lifted himself up out of his chair and immediately grabbed onto the red vinyl padding of the bar. He sidled up to the espresso machine.

"It does not work yet," he said.

"I know," I said.

He felt the metal sides and glided his hands over to the steaming rod. He gently pulled off the plastic.

"It will work tomorrow," he said. "You will come back tomorrow for *caffé*."

"I don't drink coffee," I said.

Mauro didn't seem to hear me. "You want quarters?"

"Yes," I said, thankful that he hadn't forgotten my request.

He moved to the back of the bar, his hands never leaving the red vinyl cushion. He probably had some sort of money box back there full of quarters. He bent down behind the bar and I could hear him opening a door. He rose back up and placed a small bottle filled with a bright orange liquid on the counter. I guessed he needed a refresher after such strenuous exertion.

"Here," he said, holding the bottle out to me. "Have some Crodino!" He came toward me, arm outstretched.

"Oh, no, really, I don't want . . . "

"Take it! Gratis! Free!"

I took the bottle obediently. The cap was still on so I wondered if I was supposed to just slip it into my pocket. Mauro noticed his mistake and seemed oddly embarrassed.

"Here, give it to me." He took the bottle and went back behind the bar to open it. He shuffled back toward me, but I hurried forward so he wouldn't have so far to go.

I lifted the orange liquid to my mouth, almost tasting the sweet, syrupy soda which would soon wash down my throat. I took a huge gulp, suddenly realizing that the soda was bitter. I leaned forward, wanting to spit it out. Instead, I looked at Mauro who I felt was playing a cruel joke on me.

"Good, no?" Perhaps Mauro was not fully versed in the English language, but I couldn't really believe that he didn't know the difference between a look of disgust and a look of delight.

I smiled at Mauro as best as I could. I still wanted those quarters and I knew he had them. He looked back at me and smiled. Maybe he was waiting for me to take another sip, or perhaps, to finish the whole bottle. I wouldn't be intimidated though. I just stood there and watched him, smiling, not moving an inch. Finally, it was Mauro who broke.

"Ah! Quarters!" he said, lifting his hand in the air and pointing up to the sky. Both of our smiles widened and I even brought the soda to my lips, pretending to take another sip.

"Please, sit," said Mauro, gesturing toward his chair, the only one in the place. He then turned around and went behind the bar into the back room.

I looked at the chair, but didn't dare use it. It was a commitment I wasn't quite ready to make. I walked around the room, looking for something to look at, but there really was nothing. Nothing on the walls, nothing on the built-in shelves, and nothing on the bar except for the big, silver espresso machine. Minutes passed and I decided to go ahead and sit in the chair. I would simply get up as soon as I heard Mauro shuffling back into the room.

As I stared at the shiny red vinyl of the long simulated wood paneled bar, I was strangely overcome by a heavy sleepiness. I half wondered if that bitter soda was the culprit, but before I could work myself up into a poisoned frenzy, a man walked through the door.

He wore a plaid cap, the old-fashioned kind with the top stretched out over the narrow visor. His fists were stuck deep inside the large pockets of a baseball jacket made of a thick navy wool. His pants, too, were thick, made of a light brown corduroy. The man looked at me and nodded, then looked around the room with great interest. He perused the walls, the ceiling, the shelves, seeming to see much more than I had. I wondered what Mauro would think of this unexpected boom in business. He'd probably be happy to share his bitter orange soda with someone who would really appreciate it.

Then I heard Mauro's shuffling feet. "Quarters!" I heard him say with a laugh, and then I saw his smiling round face appear at the entrance to the back room.

When Mauro saw the man with the cap and the navy blue baseball jacket, he stopped and his smile disappeared into his short black mustache. The two looked at each other for a moment, then Mauro slammed something down onto the bar and slowly walked out in front. On the bar sat an entire roll of quarters.

Once Mauro took his proprietary place in front of the bar, the other man spoke.

"*Mauro! M' ch' sfaccimma va'i fac'enno?*" The man held his palms together and shook them at Mauro, as if he were praying.

"*Faccio o' business!*" Mauro raised his hands, his thumbs gently touching the tips of his fingers, and waved them in front of the man, the back of his palms facing outwards.

Although I spoke a little Italian, these two were speaking some sort of dialect which I couldn't hope to understand. Recognizing this would be an interesting confrontation, I was happy to see these two Southern Italians would not skimp on gesticulations. And then of course, I could count on the typical Italian-American usage of the odd bit of English.

"*O' business?*" the man looked around the room with a confused expression, his palms raised in the air. "*Ma quale business?*" It seemed as if he were quite mystified that Mauro should be referring to this as a business.

"*Eh! O' my business!*" Mauro pointed to himself.

"*Ma Mauro, nun t'arricuordi cha o tuoi'o business 'acca nun o puo' fa.*" The man waved his index finger in front of Mauro, from left to right, right to left, like a parent scolding a child.

"*No, nun m'arricuordo!*" Mauro crossed his arms over his chest, clearly a show of force.

"*E nun t' passa manc' po' cazz' chill' ca dice o' Boss?*" The man seemed almost in awe of Mauro's impudence.

"*O' Boss s' po' jetta' a mmare!*" Mauro turned to the side, thumb nail to upper teeth, and flicked his whole arm forward with one swift motion. Though it was clear Mauro was not directing this mammoth insult at his visitor but rather at "o' Boss," the man seemed no less insulted.

"*Ma tu si' diventato pazzo.*" The man looked at Mauro with incredulous disgust, his hands dropped to his sides, unable to find a fitting manual reaction.

"*Eh, pazzo!*" Mauro stared at him with a maniacal smile.

The man shook his head in wonder and turned his back on Mauro. "*Tu si' pazz'!*" He turned back and looked at Mauro again, as if one more good look would somehow help him make sense of it all. But looking into Mauro's wild eyes brought no clarity to the situation. He turned back towards the door. *"Tu si proprio pazzo!"* The man brought his hands to his head and rested one on each side. He then opened the door and walked out into the sun.

Mauro stood and watched him leave, smiling madly, his arms still crossed over his chest. As he stared at the now empty space in front of him, he seemed to be mumbling to himself. Almost a minute passed and I wondered what to do. I wondered if maybe I should just leave, but then, there were still the quarters.

Finally, Mauro turned in my direction, but didn't look at me. *"Che stronzo!"* Then he looked right at me. *"Hai visto che stronzo?"* Mauro was asking me a question. It was nice that he seemed to have abandoned his dialect and was speaking to me in proper Italian, but it really didn't help.

"Eh?" he asked, waiting for an answer.

I nodded.

"Mamma mia, non ci posso credere!" Mauro started toward the bar but didn't quite know what to do.

Finally, I got up. I couldn't very well stay there all day and clearly Mauro had gone off in a direction where I simply could not follow.

"Well, I guess I'll be going," I said. I smiled at Mauro and lifted my hand in farewell.

Mauro looked up at me, truly horrified that I could even think of going. But then he seemed to realize that I was only doing what would be expected.

I walked slowly to the door, then suddenly, felt a hand on my shoulder.

"Quarters," Mauro said. He held out the entire roll to me.

I looked at him and could not help smiling. I then quickly searched my pockets for my wallet which I prayed held enough cash to cover this unexpected expense.

Mauro took hold of my arm and held me still. He placed the roll of quarters in my hand and then closed my fingers around it. "Take, please. For you. Gratis."

"Oh, but I . . . "

"Please," he said. And I realized I had better not say another word.

He took his hand off my shoulder and turned around, heading back toward his chair. He didn't seem to have any intention of bidding me a formal good-bye, so I walked out of the door in silence.

Maybe that man was right, I thought. What kind of business was this?

It was Wednesday morning at half-past seven and Johnny and I were back at the diner eating our breakfast specials. No sausage or French toast this time, just two eggs, toast and potatoes for $2.45—the early morning special.

Johnny was reading his paper as usual and I was staring at the cake carousel, mesmerized by the Black Forest which circled round and round. Next time, I thought, I'd simply order a slice of Black Forest cake for breakfast. I'd be infinitely more happy and the price would be only slightly higher.

In order to make the difficult maneuver of placing a piece of egg on his rye toast, Johnny was forced to momentarily lay down his newspaper. Rather than watching him wrestle with the unruly yoke, my eyes dropped down to the paper. "Italian," was the first word I saw, so I looked at the big, bold words which preceded and followed it. "Remains of Italian Businessman Found in East River," read the headline. I was afraid to pick up the paper and read the rest, but I did.

"Do you mind?" I asked Johnny.

He was still absorbed in his eggs. "Not at all."

"The body of Mauro Nunzio, owner of a café in Little Italy, was found yesterday near the bank of the East River," read the article. Further down it read: "The cause of death is still unknown." It was a short article, a blurb really. Clearly, they didn't know enough about the victim or the situation to give a full report.

"Johnny?"

"Yeah?"

"Remember that guy I told you about? The one that gave me the quarters?"

"Yeah?"

"He got killed."

"No way!"

"Yeah. They found him in the East River."

"Do they know who did it?"

"No."

"Man."

"Johnny."

"What?"

"I know who did it."

"Come on."

"Really. The guy that came in to talk to him. He was threatening him."

"You said they were speaking in Italian. In Neapolitan! How do you know?"

"I know! He must have been with the Mafia. He mentioned some Boss. He had to have something to do with it."

"So what do you want to do about it?"

"Go to the police."

"Now you're being ridiculous."

"I'm serious."

"And what are you going to tell them, that you saw him talking to some guy who seemed to be threatening him?"

"Exactly!"

Johnny stopped and looked at me. He didn't know where to go from there. It would be perfectly normal to report such a conversation between a murdered man and a threatening adversary. He'd have to take another tact.

"O.K., let's say that guy was from the Mafia. Let's say he was threatening this man and let's say he did kill him. So now you want to go report this guy to the police? Do you realize what you're getting mixed up in?"

I did. But then, maybe Johnny did know better. He had lived

in this neighborhood all his life. His family still owned an apartment two blocks from where we sat, although they had recently moved to New Jersey.

"I know Johnny, but what can I do? I can't just keep this to myself."

"Look, once you go pointing your finger at these kind of people, you can just forget it! You think we'd be able to stay in our apartment, in this neighborhood?"

Johnny and I had found our rent-controlled apartment through his cousin in the real estate business. It had a bedroom, living room, dining room and eat-in kitchen. We had only wished it had laundry facilities.

"So maybe we'd have to move. Isn't it worth it if this man's killer is caught?"

Johnny looked around him, as if he were searching for help. "You just don't get it do you? We wouldn't just lose the apartment. They'd be after you. Don't you see? They'd try and get you before you could testify or else they'd get you afterwards, for revenge."

I wanted to laugh at Johnny's melodrama, but somehow I knew I shouldn't.

"What do you want?" he continued. "To join some fucking witness protection program?" Johnny's voice had sunk into a fearful whisper. Maybe he felt out of control. Maybe he felt a little at my mercy.

I looked at Johnny, not knowing what else to say. I wanted to take away the fear I had caused him only moments before.

Ever since we moved to this part of town, I felt like I was living in a constant carnival, with red, white and green banners hung over the streets, hungry tourists passing through all the time, nourishing themselves on sumptuous plates of pasta and sweet creamy pastries. For Johnny, it must have been something different.

The waitress came over with a pitcher of hot water for our tea. "More hot water?" she asked.

"No," said Johnny. He couldn't even bring himself to look at her, let alone smile and call her "Bella."

I looked back down at my eggs. I realized I didn't have to eat them. I never had to eat eggs again if I didn't want to. I vowed to myself that I would never again choke down another bite. From then on, I'd only eat cake.

ETERNAL CITY

ALLISON HAD COME HOME DURING her lunch break, hoping to find the leftover lasagna in béchamel sauce her housemate had made the night before. She opened the refrigerator and, much to her surprise, found the congealed square sitting uncovered on a red plastic plate, exposed to the toxic iciness of the antique fridge. Then she remembered it was only noon. Her housemates had probably just gone down to the piazza for their morning espresso.

As she stood heating the hardened noodles in a pool of heavy cream, the phone rang. It was Stella. Stella had an appointment that night to go see an apartment, and Allison had promised she'd go with her. It's what you did, or at least what they did, Allison and Stella. They were two young American women living in a foreign land and when it came to the crucial tasks of finding a home, going to the doctor or buying a leather jacket, the two would stick together no matter the inconvenience.

"I told him we'd be there around eight. Is that O.K.?"

"Fine," said Allison. She had been settled in her place for almost a year now. "Did he sound creepy?"

"No, not exactly. It was like he was trying to sound sexy."

"Great."

"Who knows, maybe that's just how he talks," reasoned Stella.

The place was right across the river from Allison. All she and Stella would have to do was rendezvous at the old hospital floating in the middle of the Tiber, and they'd be well positioned for visiting their favorite locales, which were always filled with the friends and acquaintances—mostly acquaintances—who comprised this, their second world.

Allison's place was in the ancient Jewish ghetto, right in the center of town. How relieved she had been when she could tell her reluctant parents that she had found a spot amongst her people, just a few meters away from the famous synagogue which she had yet to visit and right next door to the old Rabbi's house which was flanked by armed guards throughout the day and night.

"Have you been to shul yet?" her father would ask hopefully.

"Maybe this Friday, Dad."

"You really ought to, Allie."

"I know." Then it came to her. "It's just that I don't have anyone to go with. It only means something when you can share it with someone."

This explanation seemed to satisfy her father.

The Romans had given the Jews this glorious little piece of the city as their home, for here was their house of worship, here were their restaurants, shops, and businesses. Why push them out into the periphery when it was so convenient to pick up their finely made textiles and their freshly baked pastries on the way home from work?

These Jews who had remained all these hundreds of years, still baking the same bread, still selling the same cloth, didn't seem much like Jews to Allison. What made a Jew a Jew in Rome? As far as Allison could surmise, it depended solely on the ability to create the perfect *carciofo alla judea*, an artichoke seared to a crisp, its leaves turned a golden brown, practically translucent as they glistened underneath a heavy coat of olive oil. She was sure the Rabbis at home would have never even heard of

136

such a thing.

Allison and Stella entered the piazza with caution, wondering which one of the massive grey buildings it could possibly be. When they realized it was the towering palazzo which commanded the central position of the intimate piazza, they turned to each other and smiled.

They found the name, Argento, on the row of buzzers and rang. A moment later, the great wooden door clicked open. The hallway was like an immense cavern, the staircase wide enough to allow for five adults walking side by side. The walls were bare, the stone under foot cold and hard, yet it had an inexplicable majesty, a home for the likes of Hannibal, not a young American woman working part time in a local pub.

They walked up slowly, ready for any of the doors which they passed to open and invite them in. But not until the last did a bespectacled head peek out, offering an enthusiastic "*Ciao*."

Stella led the way into the apartment, her eyes wandering, resting briefly on its every detail. "What an incredible place," she admired in Italian. "The moldings are fabulous."

Allison could not get over how fast Stella had mastered the Italian language. She could pull out a word like molding—*cornicone*—effortlessly, as if she'd just picked it up on some restoration site where they were piecing together the remains of a 12th-century basilica. It must have been working in the pub, thought Allison, although when would those bleary-eyed Italians be talking architectural design? Stella did say it was a pretty intellectual crowd.

Renato, that was his name, took them first to the kitchen, then through the salone and finally to Stella's would-be bedroom. There was a rather large, rickety bed sprawled out in the center, but Allison and Renato remained standing, leaning patiently against the white wall as Stella roamed around, looking in closets, examining windows, smelling curtains.

From the moment Allison had entered the apartment, she had felt Renato's heavy-lidded eyes upon her. Yes, she had felt it strongly, but had not allowed herself to believe it was true, since she had never walked into a room alongside Stella without the very opposite happening.

Estelle, as she had been christened twenty-three years earlier, had not ever allowed herself to be referred to as Stella while she lived in the United States. She had always considered it a name full of connotations of the lowliest sort: desperation, ignorance, lack of class. She felt not much different about her full name, but at least it had that going for it, being a full name. But there in Rome, Estelle had been magically reborn as Stella, Star, the name unquestionably appropriate for one whose glow seemed not to emerge from her youth, but from an impossibly distant past.

Stella had a rather paradoxical expression, her sad blue eyes curving downward, only to be lifted up by a sparkling grin which framed rows of porcelain white teeth. Her build was slight, her legs thin but strong. But her most striking feature, that which seemed to seize the attention of every man, woman, and child who crossed her path, was her hair: a mass of golden ribbons which fell in such a melodious fashion around her face, over her shoulders, and down her back. It was the kind of hair women admired as they would a luxurious mink, the kind children wished to hang from, the kind in which men desired to wrap themselves.

Allison had always been rather taken with Stella's appearance. She didn't see anything wrong in appreciating her friend for her good looks, as long as that wasn't all there was to it. Most of Allison's other friends looked just like her, medium height, brown eyes, dark brown hair, long and straight. She enjoyed spending time with someone who was different.

And Allison didn't seem to mind the fact that Stella received most all of the male attention directed their way, especially in Italy where a blonde was viewed as the manifestation of Venus on earth. Allison couldn't blame all those dark, olive-skinned men for admiring Stella's luminous aspect. They, too, wanted something different.

Renato was clearly impressed by Stella, her impeccable

Italian, her engaging personality, her striking beauty. He had already made up his mind that he would be happy to share his cherished abode with such a splendid example of American youth. It was only a matter of waiting for Stella to concur. But it was Allison who had held the opposing end of his interest, the part of him least concerned with an orderly, convenient home life.

Before a significant amount of time had passed, an amount which would have forced Allison and Renato to address each other, or at least meet eyes, the other roommate entered the bedroom. Giorgio was a tall, lanky man with a persistent smile and a goofy laugh.

"Ciao!" said Giorgio, as if to a vast roomful of close friends.

Renato greeted his roommate and immediately introduced his visitors.

"This is our potential roommate, Stella." He then turned to Allison. "And this is . . . " They hadn't yet been introduced.

"I'm nobody," said Allison. *Io sono nessuno.*

At that, Renato let out a tremendous peel of laughter, abruptly breaking the serene ambiance which had pervaded thus far. Not even the ebullient Giorgio could match his quieter roommate's hilarity. Was the very idea that this young woman before him could be referred to as "nobody" what evoked such a burst of genuine mirth, as if to emphasize that in actuality, here stood a definite somebody?

Before any more attention could be showered on this very off-handed of jokes, Allison quickly introduced herself. "My name's Allison." After that, Renato stared at her unabashedly, his half-lidded gaze now accompanied by a mischievous smile. Allison would attempt no further banter, stepping back as far as she could and allowing her friend to perform the business at hand.

Before long, Stella had established a rapport with the two men, a bond that appeared so strong, so genuine, it would have been considered a crime if any one of them had decided against Stella's moving in as soon as possible. Soon, thought Allison, these two Italians were bound to fall hopelessly in love with her.

It was all so natural for Stella, the flashing smile, the tilted head, the inviting stance, and the perfectly placed gesticulations which seemed almost to glide over her interlocutors, bringing them further and further in.

Allison recalled watching Stella with her father, when the two girls were but six years old. She sat in her father's lap, her curls tied up in huge satin bows, her arms wrapped lovingly around his neck, smothering him with kisses and being smothered with all the affection a father had to give. She laughed and smiled at him, touching his chin and his just shaven cheeks. It was a scene so foreign to Allison, she didn't know what to make of it. Where did her friend Stella get this odd mode of behavior? What attracted her to those stern eyebrows and that grey flannel lap?

"So, what'd you think?" asked Stella as they walked down the endless stone steps.

"The place is great. They seem O.K., I guess."

"Man, that Renato had a thing for you!"

"C'mon." Even with Stella, Allison felt the need to convey embarrassment. "I don't think so."

"Believe me, Allie. He could not take his eyes off of you. In fact, he didn't even bother to try."

"There was something kind of creepy about him. You know?"

"Yeah. But who knows."

"I don't know," said Allison.

Allison was scheduled to teach from nine in the morning till eight at night the next day, so she was relieved when her six o'clock lesson was canceled at the last minute. She decided to hurry over to the pub before Stella finished her shift and took off. They could have a few drinks together before dinner. She thought she still had enough pesto left over for two.

"Shouldn't you be teaching now?" asked Stella.

"The guy canceled. Thank, God. It's the one who wanted me to pose nude for him."

"He wanted to paint you or just look at you?"

"He probably just wants to see what a naked woman looks like."

"No. He probably wants to see what a naked Allison looks like," said Stella. Allison looked down.

"So, have you decided what you're going to do about the apartment?" asked Allison, trying to appear as nonchalant as possible.

"Yeah," Stella hesitated. "I actually think I'm going to take the one I saw the other day."

Allison thought maybe she hadn't properly understood. "You mean the one we saw last night, in Trastevere."

"No, the other one. I called Renato today to tell him I'm sorry."

Allison couldn't believe what she was hearing. She had simply assumed that Stella would take Renato's place, that she, Allison, would be spending time over there, eating pasta, lounging in the salone. She had envisioned it all. What was this other place Stella was choosing? She remembered no other place.

"You know, the one off of the Corso, right near your school."

"I thought you really liked that place last night. It seemed so perfect."

"Well, it's a little more expensive than I can afford and, I don't know, I thought it might be too much living with those guys. I want something a little more private I guess."

Suddenly, Allison felt strangely lost.

The cobblestones glimmered underneath the bright white lamplight as she walked through the narrow winding streets, although Allison didn't recall it ever having rained that day. It was Friday night and the neighborhood was quiet. Where else but the holy land itself would Friday night mean anything else but a night on the town. Allison was beginning to wonder how the word ghetto got such a bad name.

She arrived in front of the great synagogue and stopped, trying, as she always did, to see what was going on inside without actually entering. But nothing could be observed over those huge iron gates. One had simply to enter.

Stepping back she looked up at the towering monument, a nineteenth-century structure that paled in the presence of the great Roman amphitheater, which was its neighbor. Yet this was the place Allison's father most wanted her to visit. In a city where perfectly domed cupolas bloomed like sunflowers in an Umbrian field, she was supposed to turn her attentions to the oddly squared off roof of this unremarkable piece of infantile architecture.

This was her family's stronghold, this was where they thought Allison could replenish her spirit in a lonely, distant land. But what did those mid-western Jews know about the Eternal City anyway? They had never even been here. They had never seen the Pantheon, the great pagan temple to the gods, or the Sistine Chapel with its prophets and sibyls and old testament heroes dancing across the ceiling with beautiful bulging limbs. They had never allowed themselves to be seduced by an image, by a word or a sound which might somehow lead them astray.

She looked back up at the great synagogue, sitting safely behind rows of black bars, and could not help feeling its indifference. So she turned away, continuing on over the bridge, past the old hospital where she and Stella were to have met, into the district of Trastevere.

Allison had made a habit of spending a great deal of her time alone. She would spend hours sitting quietly in the pews of medieval churches, writing letters in elegant little cafés, sunning herself on the steps of monuments, museums, and fountains. In movie theaters, Italian couples would always take notice of what seemed to be the only single person in the house. Allison never gave it a second thought, for this was the land wherein she could do absolutely anything.

But wandering the bustling streets of Trastevere that night, Allison was overcome with a very different feeling. The thought of sitting in her favorite bar with a latte machiato or going to see the new film at the English language theater made her a little sick to her stomach. It was as if she had reached her limit, having derived all the satisfaction she could out of her admirable, yet lonely existence. She had suddenly begun to conceive of another way to live and it seemed as if there was no going back.

As she wandered aimlessly through the narrow streets, she suddenly found herself in the familiar little piazza where Stella and she had been only a few nights before. She could barely look at the huge grey building, for somehow that would be admitting something. Then she noticed the massive doors swung wide open, as if the building itself were beckoning her. Her ears strained for the sound of a party or a voice which might second the invitation, but she heard nothing. So Allison turned away and headed home.

When Stella called Allison the next day, both felt the discomfort of not having talked for almost a week.

"I'm sorry I haven't called," said Allison. "I guess I just felt like being alone."

Stella understood. "I'll be moving into my new place in a few days," she said.

Allison felt a pang of disappointment, so she said, "I'll help."

The two decided to meet for dinner that night and Allison suggested a little trattoria she had noticed in Trastevere.

It was only three in the afternoon, five hours away from dinner time. Allison figured that was just enough time for a nice walk and a cappuccino.

She walked through the ghetto, across Largo Argentina and over into Campo Di Fiori where the fruit vendors, butchers, and fish mongers were just beginning to pack away their goods. Soon the piazza, the Field of Flowers, would be given back to its rightful owners, the florists, who would fill their green buckets full of wild and vivid blooms, ready to be bought by early evening lovers. She passed through Piazza Navona and the Fountain of the Four Rivers, then over the bridge which would lead her to the Vatican.

Allison always avoided the long wide avenue which led directly to the front door of Saint Peter's. At the beginning of the road, one could see exactly where one was headed. From a distance, the grand piazza and the awesome cathedral looked like the cheap plastic miniatures the tourists bought in nearby shops. One would get closer and closer, the mammoth structure getting larger with every step, until reaching the piazza, finally being able to view its astonishing magnificence up close.

Instead, Allison preferred to approach the Vatican from the small sidestreets. This way, she would have no idea what she was about to confront until the very last moment, when all of a sudden, the enormous columns, sparkling fountains, and rows of carefully carved apostles would greet her in all their grandeur. Allison understood that sometimes, one had to carefully construct one's own surprises.

Allison strolled through the circular space of the piazza, every once in a while peeking up at the church's extraordinary façade as if she simply couldn't handle a direct, full-frontal view. Once she did allow herself a look, she was immediately drawn up the steps, into the cavernous interior of St. Peter's. Each time Allison entered the famous cathedral, she felt forced to choose but one aspect at which to direct her attention. Would it be the sweeping baroque sculptures which hung high above her head, or the restrained elegance of Michelangelo's *Pietà*? Would she stay within the wide nave, streams of afternoon light bouncing off the marble floors, or venture into the dim recesses of the private chapels where she might discover the neglected painting of a medieval master? It was all so rich and glorious to Allison, and it didn't take her long to understand how such a place might inspire a boundless faith. She even found herself wanting to sit in one of the wooden pews and pray, but she never actually did. She feared her words might reach the wrong ears. So instead she just sat and stared at the beauty which surrounded her, and her loneliness soon disappeared.

When she finally walked back out into the piazza, the sun had already begun to set. She quickly headed down the narrow alleyway which led into the district of Trastevere.

She sat down at the outdoor café next to the trattoria where she and Stella were to meet. Instead of a cappuccino, Allison ordered a prosecco, for it was already seven in the evening. Her table was surrounded by festive groups of two or more which seemed to be celebrating nothing more than the closing of the day. She sipped the dry white wine, its bubbles stinging her mouth, her tongue, her throat with a fizzy coolness. She put down her glass, content amongst her fellow revelers, and allowed herself a smile.

"Is this seat taken?" The voice came from behind, but Allison recognized it immediately, as if she were expecting him all along.

Suddenly, the tingling induced by the wine spread out all over Allison's body. She looked up at Renato's huge brown eyes which peered out from behind his wire-rimmed glasses and then immediately looked back down at the chair. No, the chair was empty and would have most likely stayed that way had Renato not come along.

"Please, go right ahead," said Allison.

"I thought I'd never see you again," he said, looking directly into Allison's eyes, that same smile on his face, as if it had never left.

"You could have asked Stella for my number." Allison was feeling bold.

"I was planning on it," replied Renato, pleasantly surprised by Allison's directness. "I hoped to meet under less formal circumstances. I didn't want to scare you." It seemed to Allison as if Renato knew himself all too well.

"Would you like something to drink?" Allison always loved to offer Italian men drinks, even though she was rarely allowed to follow through.

"I'd love it. I'll have what you're having."

Allison waved to the waiter and pointed to her glass. She then looked back at Renato. His face was soft and babyish, his round glasses making him look like an academic, but the black stubble and the golden Mediterranean tan did much to masculinize him. Then there were the eyes—those hypnotizing spheres which were constantly halved by heavy, tired lids.

Combined with his crooked smile, the left corner of his mouth just barely turned upward, his look was positively wanton.

"You're very beautiful, Allison." Allison was no longer surprised by such conversational turns, especially when uttered in a language which seemed invented for this type of passionate declaration. Still, when it came to such an utterance being directed at her, Allison always felt rather dumfounded.

"Did you just get back from work?" Allison asked, feeling no responsibility to respond directly to Renato's observation.

"Yes. I had to pick up some wine. I'm having people over tonight."

"That's nice."

"Would you like to come?"

"Oh, no. I can't."

"Why not?"

"I'm meeting someone."

"Oh."

"I'm meeting Stella," she added, not feeling the need to invent any rivals.

"You could both come."

"No, really."

Renato sat and stared at Allison until the waiter brought his drink. He took a sip, continuing to stare and then set down his glass, presumably deep in thought.

"I wonder if you would go out with me," he said.

Allison liked the fact that Renato was taking nothing for granted. "I don't know," she answered.

"I have a wonderful place I'd like to take you."

"It seems strange, I barely even know you."

"Your friend was going to be living in my apartment! Surely you could at least have dinner with me."

"All right."

"How about next Saturday night."

It was practically a week away. "O.K.," agreed Allison.

"We'll meet right here, eight o'clock."

Allison nodded her approval.

Renato got up out of his chair and bent down, kissing Allison softly on the cheek. "Till Saturday."

Once Stella arrived, Allison found herself oddly eager to tell her friend of the chance encounter.

"You just met him accidentally?" Stella's excitement shone in her wide, toothy grin.

"Yeah."

"That's so romantic."

"Oh, Stella."

"I mean it. It's fate!"

"It's really no big deal," said Allison, worried she was appearing a bit too enthusiastic. "I mean, you know these types. He's just looking for a young, easy American girl."

"And won't he be sorry!"

"I didn't say that. I just mean it's not a big deal."

"Fine. I just think you shouldn't go labeling it until at least your third date. See what happens."

On their first date he took her to a wine bar which also served food. It was a cave-like place, with only four or five tables and no sign on the door. Renato flipped through the thick black binder filled with wine labels, finally settling on a Dolcetto di Alba. When the waiter described the specials of the day, Allison chose the dish she could least understand. She wanted something made of an animal she had never even thought of eating.

They ate and they drank and Renato looked at Allison with an adoration which she had yet to comprehend. They talked, mostly about Allison, and each word brought with it the feeling that here sat a truly extraordinary woman. Even Allison had begun to believe it.

After dinner, Renato asked if he could take her to a lovely beach he knew of, not far from Rome. Allison—the warm, thick polenta sitting lightly in her stomach, the taste of heavy red wine lingering in her mouth, her head just barely floating above her neck—could not refuse.

When they arrived, Renato strategically placed their shoes

next to an abandoned boat which stood at a safe distance from the water. They walked down the beach, Renato taking Allison's hand in his own. They sat down and Allison leaned back against him. He put his arms around her from behind. She closed her eyes and listened to the water. Then Renato began speaking and she listened to him. She didn't know what he was saying, hadn't followed it from the first. But it was like music, his soft low voice whispering in her ear, words she had no need to decipher. After a while, Renato took hold of Allison's head, turned it toward him and kissed her. His mouth felt cold. She imagined that the cold night air had entered him while he was talking. As they continued to kiss, as she felt his wet mouth surrounding her own, as he moved his lips and circled his tongue and pressed her head closer to his own, slowly the chill vanished.

They began to go out every two or three days, to wine bars, restaurants and cafés, to night clubs, concerts and theaters, to museums, galleries and bookstores. He would take her to breathtaking vistas, to medieval villages, to fertile countryside. But no matter where they went, they always ended up at the same place.

At first, Renato liked to bring Allison into the salone where his roommates and friends would gather and socialize, wanting to show off his prize to the others. He would talk and laugh, wishing for Allison to join in, to say something as witty as what she had said when he first fell for her. I am nobody.

But Allison didn't want to entertain, didn't want to win anybody over. She wanted to be won. In Rome she let herself be seduced by everything, every church, fresco, or statue seemed to be vying for her attentions. And Renato, her most persistent suitor, showered her with all the pleasures Rome had to offer.

And so while Renato laughed and joked and drank, Allison would begin to yawn, and after a while she would get up with the excuse of being tremendously tired. Then she would go into Renato's bedroom and wait.

His windows opened up right onto the piazza. She leaned out, feeling the cool night breeze, listening to the diners at the restaurant below. She heard the hourly chime of the bells in the nearby church. It was midnight and the people down below were only just ordering their desserts and their liqueurs. She waited anxiously for Renato to enter the room, to feel him behind her. She wanted him to surprise her, to sneak up and grab her and hold her tight against him. For the first time in her life Allison knew what she wanted, and she desired it with a selfishness and singleness of purpose which before would have filled her with shame. It was this city, Allison thought, a city which seems to have existed forever, a city both pious and pagan, two opposing mentalities brought together by their absolute reverence of beauty.

It was Friday night and Allison and Renato were supposed to have a date, but Renato got called away on business, leaving Allison alone. She called Stella but she was busy, too.

Allison had always enjoyed those lonely nights wandering around the city, but it was different when she felt it being forced upon her. She stepped outside her front door, trying her best to forget her original plans for the evening.

She passed the old Rabbi's house, the two guards lounging around in the blue Fiat out front. Allison had always found this twenty-four hour surveillance rather extravagant, but when she considered the kind of attention and accommodations the city's most exalted Catholic figure enjoyed, this actually seemed rather paltry in comparison.

Being alone again was strange after having spent so many nights hand in hand with another, and the dark Roman streets were quickly losing their charms to a sinister presence Allison had never felt before. And so this night she did not stand outside the synagogue with her usual hesitations, but was carried in without a thought, anxious to escape her solitude.

The service had already started so she quickly found a seat on the aisle. She gazed up at the roof which was painted royal blue and covered with stars. How ugly, Allison thought, and she couldn't help feeling it deserved more—any one of the millions of frescoes which cover the walls and ceilings of the city's churches.

The cantor began singing in Hebrew, and the hard consonants and guttural sound seemed harsh and crude compared to the round Italian vowels to which Allison had grown accustomed.

Then the congregation rose and began to sing. The words were so familiar to Allison, as were the faces of the ladies, and the men's backs wrapped in white cloth. Inside, she was saying the words, in her swaying she was humming the tune. But she could not open her mouth, she could not make a sound. What was so wrong about singing this song, this song which she had sung and heard thousands of times before as a child? Here where her words were sure to reach the proper ears, Allison was mute.

There was nothing to inspire her in this white plastered hall. It was not built to overwhelm, to woo its patrons into a worshipful reverie with relics and shrines. It was not about art, or even beauty. What she saw did not carry her away into another world, what she heard only brought back memories, memories of a previous life, dull and ordinary, wrapped up in familial obligations and expectations.

As she stood motionless, hypnotized by the melodic chant, Allison felt a slight jab in her side. She turned and saw an old woman beside her, offering her a prayer book. The woman held the heavy book out to Allison, her thin arm quivering under its weight, waiting for Allison to accept, but all Allison could do was stare. The old woman pushed the book forward, *"Prendi,"* she said, but Allison could not tear her eyes away from the old woman's face, the thick brown folds of skin gathered into a look of startled puzzlement. She watched as the old woman's arm fell awkwardly to her side, her creamy grey eyes finally turning away.

"Where are we going tonight?" asked Allison.

"How about Florence?" suggested Renato.

They were in his bedroom getting ready for their night out. Allison sat in the chair by the window as Renato picked out a light cotton sweater.

"Maybe we'd better stay in the neighborhood."

Renato pulled the sweater over his head and brushed the hair out of his face. Then he walked over to Allison, lifted her up out of the chair and wrapped her in his arms.

"You don't want me to take you to Florence?"

"Maybe some other time."

He smiled at her and kissed her forehead. He kissed her cheek and then he kissed her mouth. He kept on kissing her until they fell onto the bed.

"Does this mean we're not going to dinner?" Allison smiled.

Renato kissed away her smile. Then he pulled back and looked at her.

"Listen, Renato, I need to tell you something."

"Tell me," he said.

"I've decided I need to go home." Allison said it with a surety that surprised even her.

"Home?" Renato did not know what to do with his shock.

"Back to America."

"When?"

"The end of next month."

"Why? I thought you loved it here."

"I do. It's just that this isn't my life. My life is in America. I can't pretend anymore."

"But you can make this your life, Allison. You can be wherever you want."

"It's not real, Renato. I don't know how to explain it."

"Are you leaving because of me? Because of us?"

How could he think such a thing? wondered Allison. How could he possibly think that he could have such an effect on her life. Her time with Renato was a fantasy, a dream. "Of course not," she answered.

"It's just that it seems like you're leaving just when things seem so good between us. I thought we had grown so close."

"We have," said Allison. She knew they had.

"So then why would you decide out of nowhere to leave?"

"I've got to get on with my life, Renato."

"This is your life! Rome is your home. And me. What about me?"

What about him? Allison hadn't considered Renato, hadn't expected this at all. Was there more to this than she thought? "I'm sorry, Renato."

Renato just sat and looked at her. She had made her decision. There was nothing he could do. There was nothing he could say to make her understand what she had done.

ABOUT THE AUTHOR

Molly Shapiro was born in Kansas City, Missouri. She earned her M.F.A. degree in creative writing from Columbia University, where she was the recipient of a Writing Division Fellowship. She holds a B.A. in semiotics from Brown University. *Eternal City* is her first book.

OTHER BOOKS BY HELICON NINE EDITIONS

POETRY

Prayers to the Other Life by Christopher Seid.
1996 Marianne Moore Poetry Prize winner. Selected by David Ray.

A Strange Heart by Jane O. Wayne.
1995 Marianne Moore Poetry Prize winner. Selected by James Tate.

Without Warning by Elizabeth Goldring.
Co-published with BkMk Press, University of Missouri-Kansas City.

Night Drawings by Marjorie Stelmach.
1994 Marianne Moore Poetry Prize winner. Selected by David Ignatow.

Wool Highways by David Ray.
Winner of the 1993 William Carlos Williams Poetry Award.

My Journey Toward You by Judy Longley.
1993 Marianne Moore Poetry Prize winner. Selected by Richard Howard.

Women in Cars, poems by Martha McFerren.
1992 Marianne Moore Poetry Prize winner. Selected by Colette Inez.

Hoofbeats on the Door by Regina deCormier.
Introduction by Richard Howard.

Black Method by Biff Russ.
1991 Marianne Moore Poetry Prize winner. Selected by Mona Van Duyn.

FICTION

Nice Men and Good Girls, stories by June Spence.
1995 Willa Cather Fiction Prize winner. Selected by Leonard Michaels.

Knucklebones, short stories by Annabel Thomas.
1994 Willa Cather Fiction Prize winner. Selected by Daniel Stern.

Galaxy Girls:Wonder Women, stories by Anne Whitney Pierce.
1993 Willa Cather Fiction Prize winner. Selected by Carolyn Doty.

Return to Sender, a first novel by Ann Slegman.

The Value of Kindness, short stories by Ellyn Bache.
1992 Willa Cather Fiction Prize winner. Selected by James Byron Hall.

Italian Smoking Piece (with Simultaneous Translation) by Christy Sheffield-Sanford.
A series of twenty meditations.

Sweet Angel Band, short stories by R. M. Kinder.
1991 Willa Cather Fiction Prize winner. Selected by Robley Wilson.

ANTHOLOGIES

Spud Songs: An Anthology of Potato Poems (Proceeds to Benefit Hunger Relief).
Edited by Gloria Vando and Robert Stewart.

Poets at Large: 25 Poets in 25 Homes (Commemorating National Poetry Month).
Edited by H.L. Hix.

The Helicon Nine Reader: A Celebration of Women in the Arts. (The best of *Helicon Nine*, the Journal of Women's Arts & Letters.) Edited by Gloria Vando Hickok.